GW00459339

A Murderous Season

The Admiral Shackleford Mysteries Book 3

Beverley Watts

BaR Publishing

Cover design by Karen Ronan: www.coversbykaren.com

Contents

Chapter One

'You'd think we'd be able to see a bloody lighthouse from miles away,' muttered the Admiral.

'Well, it can't be too far Sir,' Jimmy responded mildly as he fiddled with his iphone, trying unsuccessfully to get a signal.

'This is what comes with relying on technology,' Mabel declared loftily from the back. 'We never had any of these problems when we used maps.'

'Unless you were the one reading the map,' mumbled the Admiral under his breath.

'I have to say I'm actually very excited,' offered Emily, 'I've never stayed in a lighthouse before.'

'Neither has ninety nine percent of the population,' commented the Admiral sourly, 'Because most of 'em have got better sense.'

'Bingo,' declared Jimmy, his head stuck so far through the window that only his rear end and legs were still inside the car.

'I can't drive off with you hanging out of the car window Jimmy.'

'It'll be okay if you go slowly Sir,' Jimmy threw behind him. 'If I come back in, we might never get the signal back and time's getting on if we want to get to get there before dark.'

'What a bloody cake and arse party,' Charles Shackleford muttered, putting the car in gear and pulling slowly forward.

'I THINK IT SAYS TO TAKE THE NEXT TURNING ON THE RIGHT,' yelled Jimmy breathlessly, gripping onto the edge of the window with one hand and holding the phone out with the other.

'WHAT DO YOU MEAN YOU THINK?' the Admiral shouted back, glancing over at the small man, and very nearly giving him an impromptu lobotomy as the car accidently swerved towards the hedge.

'I CAN'T HEAR WHAT THAT CHAP'S SAYING AND I CAN'T SEE THE SCREEN VERY WELL WITHOUT MY GLASSES,' Jimmy yelled, 'I THINK THEY MIGHT BE IN THE GLOVE COMPARTMENT.'

'HERE, YOU CAN BORROW MINE LOVE,' Emily offered. She unclipped her seat belt and wound down the back window intending to lean out and hand them to Jimmy. Unfortunately, as she leaned forward and held the glasses out, Pickles, the Admiral's elderly Springer spaniel, who up until then had been sitting quietly in between her and Mabel, decided that the pungent smell of manure wafting into the back was simply too much. With a joyful bark, he clambered onto Emily's knee and stuck his head out of the open rear window.

In that moment three things happened. Emily's glasses went flying into the hedgerow, never to be seen again and in the updraft created by the movement of the car, Pickles' excited drool smacked Jimmy squarely in the eye as they came face to face.

Recoiling, Jimmy lost his tenuous grip on the edge of the passenger door and pitched headfirst towards the tarmac. Just in time, the Admiral lunged towards the small man and managed to grab hold of his left foot.

The ladies screamed, Jimmy yelped, the Admiral swore, Pickles barked, and the car gave a horrible whining sound as it ended up in a ditch...

In contrast to the earlier pandemonium, there was total silence as the car juddered to a halt right next to the hedge. Shaken, but fortunately uninjured, Jimmy slithered the rest of the way down onto the grass before climbing to his feet. Puffing and panting, he leaned forward and peered inside the car at the shocked faces of its occupants. Then he glanced down at his phone, miraculously still in his hand and said weakly, 'I think I've got a signal now Sir.'

'I can't imagine how you managed to end up in a ditch on a road as slow as this one,' commented the mechanic matter of factly when he arrived an hour later. Seventy if he was a day, the man wore overalls that looked as though the last time they'd seen a washing machine was back in the nineteen fifties.

'Now if you'd gone over the cliff at Lammas Lane, that I could have understood,' he continued conversationally, proclaiming himself a local. 'I mean a forty-foot drop with no fence between the road and the edge, now there's a challenge.'

'We wouldn't really have need of your services if we'd been foolish enough to have strayed over the edge of a cliff,' answered Emily primly, clearly less than impressed with their knight in shining armour.

'So, can you pull the bollocking car out of the ditch or not before we all freeze to death?' butted in the Admiral tetchily.

The mechanic sighed and looked up at the rapidly darkening sky, then back at his tow truck which also looked as though it had stepped out of an episode of *The Darling Buds of May*. Then he shook his head regretfully. 'Too late for that now,' he proclaimed apologetically, 'It'll have to wait 'til morning.'

'Well you can't just leave us here,' exclaimed Mabel slightly panic stricken at the thought of spending the night sitting in the back of the car, 'Charlie thinks we could freeze to death.'

The mechanic frowned. 'Where are you headed?' he asked after a moment.

'Whitebeam Lighthouse' responded Jimmy eagerly.

'Well that's only over yonder hill,' their rescuer offered, 'You could walk it in no time.'

'Not with the six ton of bloody luggage we've got with us,' argued the Admiral. He paused before continuing grudgingly, 'If you could see your way to giving us a lift, Mr... er.... we'd be happy to pay you a bit extra. All in the spirit of Christmas.' The mechanic's eyes narrowed. 'Cash of course,' the Admiral offered between gritted teeth. There was a brief pause, then the mechanic nodded his head and put out his hand.

'Name's Arthur, but everyone round here calls me Mack... 'cos I'm a mechanic,' he added helpfully...

Ten minutes later they were wedged like sardines in the cab of

Mack's truck while the mechanic negotiated hairpin bends with a nonchalance born of familiarity.

'Can't understand why anybody would want to stay in a lighthouse,' commented Mack as the landscape opened up in front of them revealing a stormy sea and a cliff top road every bit as precarious as he'd predicted. 'You mark my words,' he continued, swinging the truck onto the road without noticeably slowing down. Mabel gave a small scream and Emily closed her eyes. 'You'll have had enough by tomorrow morning. The stairs'll be the death of you, that's for sure.'

'That's if the bloody road and his bloody driving don't do for us first,' muttered the Admiral under his breath.

'Look,' commented Emily excitedly, finally plucking up the courage to open her eyes, 'There's Whitebeam lighthouse now. Ooh,' she squealed delightedly, clapping her hands, 'it looks just like something out of *The French Lieutenant's Woman.*'

'I wouldn't know,' offered Mabel disapprovingly, 'I've never watched a pornographic film.'

The other three looked at her in astonishment, but as Jimmy opened his mouth to explain, Mack shook his head and said, 'A bloody horror film would be more appropriate given the number of people that have chosen to end it all by throwing themselves out of the lantern room. Why only last week a local girl was found on the pavement outside the front door.'

'Oh my goodness,' breathed Mabel faintly.

'That's dreadful,' added Emily, eying the approaching lighthouse with trepidation.

'What happened?' asked the Admiral leaning forward with interest.

'How do you know she jumped?' interjected Jimmy before Mack had a chance to speak.

'She left a note,' offered Mack matter of factly. 'Her body was found by a couple who'd turned up to rent the place. Needless to say they didn't stay very long.'

'What was she doing in the lighthouse in the first place?' the Admiral asked.

'Cleaner,' responded Mack. 'She used to pretty the place up in between guests. Apparently, the note said something along the lines that she couldn't live without her mum or summat like that.'

'What happened to her mum?' Jimmy couldn't help asking.

'Disappeared about five years ago. Left poor old Jenny with her stepdad.' Mack shrugged, finally slowing the truck as they approached the lighthouse.

'Could her mother have been murdered?' the Admiral questioned eagerly.

Mack shrugged again, concentrating on the less than level road that wound up to the white monolith, now looming up in front of them, ghostly in the winter twilight. Bringing the truck to a halt, he sat back and turned towards his passengers who made no move to get out. All four of them were looking at him expectantly.

'The police were suspicious if I remember rightly,' the mechanic commented eventually when it became clear they were staying put until he'd given them the rest of the story. 'But they didn't find a body. Poor old Jenny was distraught at the time. She didn't get on with her stepdad

'To be honest no-one really believed her mum had upped and left her, I mean it's not a normal thing for a mum to do is it? But there wasn't enough evidence to point the finger at anybody.' With a heartfelt sigh, he opened the door and climbed out of the truck indicating the conversation was at an end.

With barely restrained excitement, the Admiral glanced over at Jimmy before pushing Pickles off his lap and clambering out to help Mack lift off their luggage.

'I'll pick up your car in the morning,' Mack said once everything had been unloaded, then I'll pop over and give you the bad news tomorrow evening.' He paused and stared at the Admiral expectantly until the latter sighed and put his hand in his pocket.

'Don't fall down the stairs mind and best to stay out of the lantern tower – we don't want to be scraping any of you up off the tarmac,' was Mack's cheerful parting shot as he turned the truck round and drove off.

The wind was picking up and the lighthouse brooded over the

shadowy landscape. They could hear the sea crashing against the rocks below. Emily shivered while Mabel fumbled about for the keys she'd been sent.

'Come on old girl,' Jimmy said encouragingly, 'You'll be snug and warm in no time. Let's get inside and put the kettle on.'

'Bugger the kettle,' announced the Admiral gleefully, picking up his and Mabel's cases, 'I think a tot of the hard stuff's called for.' Marching up the steps, he plonked the cases down and turned back to the other three trailing slowly after him. 'Come on you lot, get a shift on. What are you – bloody geriatrics? There's not a moment to lose if we don't want the trail to get colder than it already is.'

'What trail?' asked Mabel plaintively, 'I really don't feel up to a walk in the dark Charlie. It's far too cold and we don't want to fall off the edge of a cliff on our first night.'

'I don't really fancy falling off the edge of a cliff on our last night either,' muttered Emily tartly, taking hold of her friend's arm to help her up the steps.

'What the bloody hell are you on about Mabel?' questioned the Admiral waiting impatiently for Jimmy to unlock the door. 'We're not walking anywhere tonight. I'm talking about the case.

'*Operation Lighthouse* is on...'

Chapter Two

The ground floor of the lighthouse was barely twenty five feet in diameter and was dominated by a large spiral staircase that wound right up to the top.

All four stared silently up at the steep stairs. Pickles whined softly.

'The living accommodation is on the first floor,' offered Jimmy helpfully glancing down at the brochure.

'I'm not sure I can go up and down those stairs for five days Charlie,' whispered Mabel anxiously. 'I'll be laid up for Christmas Day.'

'Well, it's your bloody fault we're here in the first place,' commented the Admiral unsympathetically, 'and you've got to go up and down 'em at least until the car's fixed – unless you want to sleep here.' He looked round the bare room with a slight shudder. 'Bloody draughty if nothing else.' Then he hefted one of the suitcases and started up the stairs, Pickles close on his heels.

'I won a competition,' protested Mabel, gripping hold of the banister as if her life depended on it.

'You were probably the only daft bugger who entered it,' the Admiral threw back, as he stopped for a breather.

'Well I still think it's exciting,' commented Emily, touching her friend's shoulder encouragingly. 'Don't worry Mabel dear, I'm right behind you.' It was unclear what she actually intended to do should her friend lose her footing. The likelihood was that both would end up in a heap at the bottom of the stairs.

Watching apprehensively from the first step, Jimmy decided to stay put until he was sure that both ladies had made it safely to the first floor. At least he'd provide a slightly softer landing than the concrete floor…

In the end it took another twenty minutes for them to finally get themselves and all their luggage up to the first floor which fortunately was much cosier than the entrance hall below.

The room was dominated by a huge Christmas tree beautifully decorated with a myriad of twinkling lights and there was a delightful artificial fire burning merrily in the grate. Clearly the owner had managed to find another cleaner and had gone overboard to ensure the room was warm and inviting with a true Christmassy feel. Of course, there's nothing like a gruesome murder to put a damper on the festive spirit.

Unfortunately, the seasonal cheer was currently lost on its latest occupants who had finally collapsed gasping into the comfortable sofas strategically arranged so that each piece of furniture was only a few steps away from the staircase.

'No wonder so many people come to a sticky end in this place,' wheezed the Admiral when he finally managed to speak.

'Perhaps we should find somewhere else to stay,' commented Jimmy with a concerned look at his former commanding officer's red perspiring face. Emily and Mabel nodded in agreement, still too out of breath to speak.

'Nonsense,' grunted the Admiral to the other three's amazement. 'It will do us all good to get a bit of exercise.' The large man leaned forward. 'A young girl fell to her death from within these very walls,' he huffed, 'and I say it's fate that sent us here so we can find out what really happened to her and her mother.'

'We won't be much good to her or fate if we end up in matching plots,' commented Jimmy drily.

'Mabel, did I tell you we've got a couple of nice spots picked out in Dartmouth cemetery?' Emily interrupted. 'We got a very good deal didn't we Jimmy – buy one, get one free.'

'Really?' said Mabel, immediately forgetting her tiredness, 'How on earth did you manage that?'

'We cut a coupon out of the newspaper. We chose two nice plots near to that large oak tree just past the entrance,' explained Emily, 'so we'll get a bit of shade in the summer.'

'What do you think Charlie, shall we see if we can get a coupon? I mean we don't want to leave it until all the nice spots have been taken.'

'What a load of old bollocks – matching plots? I don't care if they plant me upside down on a council tip,' the Admiral commented bluntly, 'As long as they wait until I'm bloody dead.'

'Which might be sooner than you think,' muttered Emily darkly.

'I think we need to decide who's going to sleep in the top room,' Jimmy butted in hastily, after glancing over at his wife's mutinous expression. 'To be fair Sir, as you're the one who had a heart attack only a couple of years ago, I really think you and Mabel should take the room on the next floor and Emily and I will take the Tower suite.'

Drawing himself up pompously the Admiral opened his mouth to argue that as the senior ranking member of the party, it stood to reason that he should be the one housed in the best room. Climbing to his feet, he made his way over to the staircase and looked up. The third floor wasn't even visible from this angle. Frowning, he coughed and hurriedly added that in the interests of group moral and the importance of giving subordinates the occasional reward for first-rate execution of orders, he would, on this occasion, allow Jimmy and Emily to take the suite...

Sitting at the sunny dining table with a large plate of toast and marmalade the next morning went a long way to improving the Admiral's mood. As long as they came down with everything they were likely to need until it was time to go back to bed, Charles Shackleford reasoned that they had every expectation of surviving Mabel's prize holiday. Unfortunately, they were only on their second cup of tea when his beloved discovered she'd left her blood pressure pills on the bedside table.

As he watched his former commanding officer turn an interesting shade of purple, Jimmy hastily offered to go up and fetch them.

'While you're up there Jim, can you bring me my bunion cream from the bathroom,' Emily called after him as the small man started up the stairs. Turning to Mabel, she lifted her leg up towards the table and continued, 'Have you ever seen anything quite like that Mabel dear,' she asked proudly pointing towards the large red lump on the side of her foot.

The Admiral, who was wondering whether he could manage a third piece of toast, on finding himself face to face with Emily's big toe, promptly decided he'd had enough. Mabel shook her head in wide eyed awe and declared gravely that indeed she couldn't ever remember seeing quite such an impressive protuberance.

'Would you like any more tea my dear?' butted in Jimmy breathlessly after returning in super quick time with Mabel's pills and his wife's bunion cream. Emily eyed him narrowly. His prompt return had prevented her from giving a graphic description of her doctor's proposal for the lump's removal. Then she sniffed and held out her cup.

'So, what's the plan?' continued Jimmy jovially, ignoring his wife's daggered looks. If he'd allowed Emily free reign when it came to her bunion, the rest of them were unlikely to want to eat again for the rest of the day.

'Thought we'd have a bit of a scout about,' the Admiral responded in a tone that brooked no argument. 'We won't have the car, but the village isn't very far away and it's nice and crisp out. We can grab a bit of scran and ask a few preliminary questions about our dead cleaner's missing mother. Besides, it'll do us good to have a spot of exercise and I'm sure Pickles fancies a walk,' he added to head off any thoughts of possible mutiny.

Pickles chose that moment to utter a loud snore, contentedly replete after consuming the plate of leftover toast along with a bowl of milky tea, declaring to all and sundry exactly what his opinion was regarding his master's proposal.

In the end it took them nearly an hour to get to the local village of Morwelly after they elected to follow the more scenic north Devon coastal path that ran parallel to the road. In the beginning both Emily and Mabel had waxed lyrical about the myriad of beautiful colours created by the sea crashing majestically onto the rocks below them. But after the third hill, they subsided into grim silence, and by the time the four reached the outskirts of the village, the only one still speaking to the Admiral was Pickles, and to be fair, the spaniel didn't really have much to say. However, his wagging tail spoke volumes about his assessment of their 'spot of exercise'.

'At least someone enjoyed it,' was Emily's only curt statement as they stumbled into the first tearoom they came to.

Sinking into the chair, Mabel fanned herself vigorously with the menu. 'I swear you're trying to kill me off,' she muttered. 'But I'm giving you fair warning Charlie Shackleford, if you make me walk any further, it'll be your murder under investigation…'

Chapter Three

H alf an hour later, fortified by a large latte along with a piece of homemade Christmas cake that would have fed an entire family during the war, their individual moods gradually improved as did their ability to speak until eventually the Admiral was back to his normal brusque self as evidenced by the question he put to their waitress.

'You didn't happen to know that girl who took a flying lesson off the top of Whitebeam lighthouse did you?'

The waitress stared incredulously at him for a few seconds as if she couldn't believe someone could be quite so insensitive, while the other three squirmed uncomfortably. Then, picking up their empty cups, she said curtly, 'If you're talking about Jenny Welbeck, yes I did know her. She happened to be my best friend.'

'We're so very sorry for your loss,' murmured Emily glaring at the Admiral as she leaned forward to put out a sympathetic hand. The waitress's features softened and her eyes filled with tears as she put their empty cups onto her tray.

'It must have been a terrible shock,' added Mabel compassionately, 'I can't imagine how it must have felt and what possible reason such a young girl could have for ending her own life.'

'She was upset about her mum,' commented the waitress, pointedly ignoring the Admiral.

'We were told her mother just upped and left one day. It's hard to imagine any woman walking away from her child,' said Jimmy gently with a warning glance towards his former commanding officer who'd just opened his mouth.

The waitress shook her head and rummaged around for a tissue in her apron. 'Jenny never believed for one second that her mother would have willingly left her with her stepdad, she continued after blowing her nose, 'Not for any reason.'

'So, what do you think happened to her mother?' asked Emily softly.

'I think she was murdered, that's what I think. And I know for a fact that Jenny thought so too. She told the police and everything. Jenny bloody hated her stepdad.'

'Perhaps she was still struggling to come to terms with what happened,' suggested Mabel.

The waitress shook her head sadly. 'I really thought she was finally getting over it. We were supposed to be going to see *Take That* in Plymouth. I know she'd been a bit down lately, and I know she thought about her mum all the time, but I can't believe she actually thought life wasn't worth living anymore. There's no way she'd have missed the opportunity to see Mark Owen in the flesh. She was obsessed by him.'

She sniffed as she began to stack their plates. 'It makes no sense. Why didn't she speak to me if something was bothering her? I can't help but wonder whether someone pushed her off that bloody lighthouse.'

'Did you tell the police all this?' asked Jimmy with a frown.

'Of course I did,' she answered indignantly. 'They weren't interested. Her stepdad got to them first. He told them she'd been depressed. Said he wasn't surprised she'd done herself in. But I knew her better than he ever could, and she might have been a bit down, but it was probably because she was living with him. Whatever, that bastard said, I just can't get my head around her actually killing herself. She only had to stick it out another year because she was going to uni next September. Believe me, she couldn't wait.'

'So, do you think the same person could have killed her and her mother?' interrupted the Admiral, unable to keep silent any longer.

The waitress looked at him with dislike. 'I have no idea,' she answered tersely, 'and I can't stand here gossiping all day with the likes of you, so you'll have to excuse me.' Picking up the tray she turned her back and walked briskly towards the kitchen.

'Honestly Charlie you can be such an obnoxious old fart sometimes,' said Emily when the waitress was out of earshot.

'Well we know a lot more than we did when we started,' declared the Admiral defensively.

'That's no thank to you,' retorted Mabel, getting to her feet. 'You think you're so clever Charlie Shackleford, but sometimes you're nothing but a liability.' After giving him one last glare, she pushed her chair back and made her way to the ladies followed closely by Emily who made sure to offer the Admiral her own parting scowl.

The two men sat in silence for a few minutes, then the Admiral sighed. 'Sometimes Jimmy lad, I just don't understand women. They just don't grasp that you've got to be up-front to get to the meat and two veg of the matter. It's no good pussy footing round the bloody houses.'

Jimmy sighed. 'I quite agree Sir that direct questioning is very often the best way to get answers,' the small man said carefully, 'but occasionally it has to be said you have a tendency to be the human equivalent of a social hand grenade... Sir.'

The Admiral glared at his former Master at Arms in indignation. If they'd been at home, Jimmy would have been given two hours dishwasher duty and no mistake. However, before he could tear a strip off his out of line subordinate, the two ladies arrived back at the table.

'What's our next move then Mr. No-It-All,' asked Emily sarcastically, sitting back down.

The Admiral glanced down at his watch. It was just after ten thirty. 'Well,' he mused, 'We've got an hour or so before we can wet our whistle at the pub and get a spot of scran, so what do you say we have a look round the village and see if they've got a library? They might carry back copies of the local newspaper and there's bound to be a story about young Jenny Welbeck popping her clogs. We might even be able to find out some intel on her mother.'

Emily sniffed but couldn't find anything amiss with the

Admiral's suggestion, so they paid up and headed out into the late morning sunshine.

'What are we going to do with Pickles while we're in the library?' asked Mabel bending down to give the springer a fuss.

'We'll find him a nice patch of sun to bask in and he'll be right as rain,' the Admiral responded as they made their way towards what looked to be a village green dominated by a huge Christmas tree in its centre. The cottages surrounding it, while not quite as chocolate box as in South Devon, were quaint enough. The North Devon coast was much wilder, and the grey stone of the houses reflected the need to stand up to any inclement weather.

They spent a pleasant half an hour wandering around the edge of the small green and the narrow cobbled streets beyond until at length they found themselves back where they'd started. While the village boasted a convenience store and gift shop, two coffee shops and a pub, there didn't appear to be a library. When Mabel and Emily finally questioned a pleasant lady behind the counter at the convenience store, they were informed that the nearest one was in Ilfracombe five miles away.

'Well that's put paid to that,' was the Admiral's frustrated comment as they came out.

'We'll have to wait until we get the car back,' added Jimmy, 'and hope they don't take too long with it. We've only got five days after all. We might just have to sit this one out Sir.'

The Admiral frowned, unwilling to admit that they'd hit a brick wall. 'We've got the internet back at the lighthouse, haven't we?' questioned Emily who hated to see a job unfinished. 'I've brought my tablet and there might be something about it on that Goggle thing.'

The Admiral brightened and nodded his head enthusiastically. 'And meanwhile, where's the next best place to get intel?' The other three looked at him nonplussed and the large man shook his head at their obtuseness. 'The pub of course,' he said finally when they continued to look at him blankly. 'And there just happens to be one not fifty yards away. Lead the way Jimmy lad.'

The Red Lion was almost empty as the lunchtime rush hadn't

yet started and they hesitated on the threshold, debating whether to sit inside or out to take advantage of the brief winter sun. In the end they opted for inside reasoning that they'd probably find more locals to question. The interior was dimly lit and had the vague smell of hops that seemed to characterise all British pubs, especially when they were empty. The décor was all blackened wooden beams and the room sported a huge stone fireplace in the corner. There was a roaring fire blazing merrily in the grate casting a welcome glow over the room and everywhere was either covered in fake snow or wreathes of holly, resembling a scene out of *A Christmas Carol*. Jimmy half expected to see Ebenezer Scrooge walk through the door at any moment.

Fifteen minutes later they were cosily - and more important, strategically - ensconced in a corner table facing out into the room. The pub quickly began to fill up and by twelve thirty the last free table had been taken.

'Right then,' declared the Admiral downing the last of his pint. 'I think it's time to grab another pint and some scran along with a spot of interrogation. 'You up for it Jimmy lad?' At the small man's nod, Charles Shackleford climbed out of their booth and headed determinedly towards the bar.

Three of the four tall stools fronting the gnarled oak counter were already taken and the Admiral nodded towards the elderly occupants enjoying their first pint of the day. 'We'll start there, Jimmy. If this place is anything like the Ship, those old timers'll definitely be able to point us in the right direction.'

Without waiting for his friend, the Admiral strode purposefully towards the gap nearest his potential informants. Hurrying after him, Jimmy couldn't help but wince at the outraged glares directed at his former commanding officer's back as the large man elbowed anyone in his path – much in the way of a rugby prop forward. Charles Shackleford was of course completely oblivious.

The barman was young, barely out of nappies in the Admiral's opinion, and he sported a black tea shirt with the slogan *Pub of the year, 1705.*

'I'll have another two pints of your local, two Prows Echoes and four scotch eggs,' he announced without waiting to be asked. The young barman stared at him for a second, possibly in shock at his abrupt appearance.

'Preferably before you have to start shaving,' the Admiral continued loudly as the barman looked uncertainly towards muttering customers who had been waiting patiently to be served for the last ten minutes. Then, no doubt recognising the type of customer it was in his best interest to get rid of as soon as possible, the barman gave his audience a small apologetic smile and hurried to comply.

As he waited, the Admiral wasted no time clambering up onto the empty bar stool and introducing himself to the customer sitting next to him. In contrast to the barman, the man was so old, the Admiral couldn't help but wonder how the bloody hell he'd actually managed to climb on to the stool in the first place. For a couple of seconds, Charles Shackleford thought perhaps he'd dropped a bit of a bollock with his choice of mole, but the watery blue eyes that turned towards him in response to his greeting were fortunately full of lively intelligence. 'Charles Shackleford,' the Admiral announced with a flourish, thrusting out his hand.

'It's bloody packed in here,' the old man responded loudly ignoring the Admiral's proffered hand.

'It's all about the money nowadays. Mind, you, should have been here during the war. Couldn't move for bloody yanks.' The Admiral frowned, wondering what on earth the old fella was talking about. But his potential informant hadn't finished. 'Now it's all bloody tourists wanting poncy pub food and bugger the regulars.' He raised his eyebrows obviously waiting for the Admiral to comment. Uncharacteristically Charles Shackleford, well aware he was one of the bloody tourists in question, didn't have a quick response and it was left to Jimmy to step into the breach.

'It's the same down our neck of the woods,' the small man mourned, taking his newly poured pint off the bar and stepping closer to the old man's stool. 'Can't go for a quiet pint without tripping over the damned grockles. Would I be right in guessing you're one of the only regulars in here Sir?'

The old man nodded solemnly and finished the rest of his pint before looking at the Admiral and Jimmy expectantly. 'Another pint of your local,' the Admiral said plonking his newfound friend's glass on the counter loudly, totally oblivious to the fact that the barman had moved onto another customer.

'Apart from this miserable pair sitting next to me,' the old man muttered, with a disparaging nod towards his two silent companions, 'there's just me and Willy Welbeck. I'll have a packet of crisps as well. Salt and vinegar.'

'Welbeck, name ring a bell?' the Admiral murmured to Jimmy in his version of sotto voce, which of course meant that everyone in a ten feet radius heard him.

'What do you gents want with old Willy?' the old man asked suspiciously, snatching the proffered bag of crisps out of the barman's hand.

The Admiral made an effort to shrug nonchalantly and composed his face into an expression he felt was more fitting when talking about the recently bereaved. 'We heard he'd recently lost his stepdaughter. Very sad state of affairs.'

'Shouldn't think he lost much sleep,' responded the old man liberally spraying the Admiral and Jimmy with chewed up bits of potato. 'They didn't get on at all. Jenny thought her stepdad was responsible for her mum vanishing.'

The Admiral made a concerted effort to compose his expression into one of mild interest with an undertone of faint sadness. 'So, her mother disappeared, did she? Must have been hard on the poor girl. Was it long ago?'

'Question you should be asking is did she go willingly or was she helped on her way if you get my drift?' replied their informant, while looking meaningfully at his already empty pint glass. The Admiral sighed. It was a good job he was so in tune with his public duty, at this rate he'd have to take out a mortgage just to pay for the bloody beer.

'It happened about five years ago,' the old man continued. 'She just disappeared one night. Never found out for sure what happened to her. The police never found a body.' He took a satisfied sip of his pint then turned and nudged his companion sitting silently on the stool next to him.

'Here Neville, can you remember what happened when Debra Welbeck disappeared?' He turned back to the Admiral and Jimmy adding in a loud whisper, 'Can't remember his own bloody name half the time, but if you catch him on a good day you can get a bit o' sense out of him.'

The three of them stared expectantly at Neville who at first didn't appear to have heard them. After about a minute and a half, just as the Admiral thought he couldn't stand it any longer, Neville turned towards them and croaked, 'Not rightly...' They waited for a few seconds for him to say more, but that appeared to be it. Shaking his head, Neville turned back to his pint.

'If I was a betting man, I'd wager that's all you'll be getting from him today,' said his companion to the disappointed duo beside him. 'But if you're interested, you could always get it straight from the horse's mouth.' He nodded towards a man sitting alone in the far corner of the bar. 'That's old Willy Welbeck. Comes in every day. Reckon he's got nothing else to do. There ent much call for boat trips this time o' year.' The Admiral and Jimmy turned in unison to stare over at their prime suspect. He was large with a ruddy face under a shock of white hair. But it was his hands that caught their interest as they watched him pick up his pint. They looked as though they belonged to a navvy. Easily capable of squeezing the life out of somebody and disposing of the body.

'Well he certainly looks capable,' murmured Jimmy eying the goliath a little apprehensively.

'Like I said, they never found a body,' their elderly companion repeated. 'Young Jenny told everyone who'd listen that he'd buried her mother under the patio, but the police never found anything despite digging up the whole bloody garden.

'According to Willy, his stepdaughter was just out of her mind with grief and couldn't accept that her mother had run out on them both.' He drank the last of his pint and looked over at the Admiral hopefully. Charles Shackleford narrowed his eyes, debating whether their informant had outlived his usefulness. From the corner of his eye he could see Mabel and Emily signalling the arrival of their scotch eggs, but there was always the off chance he and Jimmy might need to question their mole again at a later date. This detective lark was proving bloody expensive. In the end however, he sighed resignedly and signalled to the barman to pull another pint.

Chapter Four

A half an hour later, the Admiral sighed and patted his stomach contentedly.

'Well that filled a hole nicely. Much better than that bloody bunny grub you keep feeding me Mabel.'

'That bunny grub as you call it is the only way you can still squeeze into your trousers Charlie Shackleford. It's either salad twice a week or you give up the beer.'

The Admiral shuddered. He never thought he'd see the day when he'd think longingly of his daughter Victory's cooking, but once Mabel had got her feet under the table at the Admiralty, it had to be said he found himself more often than not on the wrong end of an ear pounding. Hurriedly he finished his pint on the off chance she decided to cut down on his daily intake immediately. Not beyond the realms of possibility. Determining a change of subject was definitely in order, he placed his empty glass decisively on the table, and took out his notepad and pen. They'd finished their scran, so it was high time they had a conflab.

'Right then, what do you think?' He looked round at the other three who sat in various stages of perplexity. Apart from Emily who looked as though she'd swallowed a camel.

'It was very nice but a bit rich I'd say.'

'I think the scotch egg might have given me a spot of wind.'

'I enjoyed the chips though.'

Charles Shackleford sighed in frustration. It was like pulling teeth. 'I meant about the case, not the bloody food.'

'Oh, right then,' Jimmy quickly jumped in. 'Well Sir, we know that Jenny Welbeck fell from the lantern tower just over a week ago...'

'Or she was pushed,' interrupted the Admiral darkly.

'Or pushed,' Jimmy agreed. 'But in all honesty Sir, we haven't actually found any evidence that she might have been helped out of the tower window. Everything we've been told so far is no more than conjecture.

'What we really need to do is to get into the lantern tower and have a recce, see if there's anything the plod missed. After all, they weren't really looking for foul play so they might well have overlooked something important.'

The Admiral nodded his head, determinedly avoiding the thought of the number of stairs involved in Jimmy's proposed recce. Instead he said, 'We need to have a chat with our friend Willy without letting on why we're interested.'

'How about we try and book a boat trip?' Jimmy answered. 'He's unlikely to be booked up. That old fella mentioned there wasn't much call for them this time of year.'

'Because there aren't many people daft enough to want one,' butted in Emily with a shudder. 'You can count me out of any potential onboard shenanigans Jimmy.'

'You're the President of *Ladies Afloat*,' commented Mabel.

Emily sniffed. 'I'm always up for a quick trip round Dartmouth Harbour with a large gin and tonic. In the *summer*. But it'll be freezing out there, you know it will.'

'We won't actually go out on his boat unless we don't have a choice,' the Admiral responded, with a frown at Emily's foot-dragging. 'We'll just sort of arrange it.' He leaned forward before continuing furtively, 'We'll wait here until old Willy legs it, then we'll follow him, see where his place is.'

'What if he doesn't go to his boat shed?' Jimmy asked, wincing at the Admiral's version of a stage whisper. 'I mean, he might just be going home.'

'Don't put a spanner in the works Jimmy lad,' said the Admiral, waving away Jimmy's misgivings. 'We'll make it up as we go along. We're pretty much experts at this whole stake out business now.'

'Do you think we should order one in for dinner tonight?' asked Mabel. 'I quite fancy a nice bit of beef, and it'll save us cooking Emily.'

There was a short silence while the other three searched for a response. Luckily the object of their discussion chose that particular moment to walk past their table.

'That's our cue Jimmy,' puffed the Admiral, struggling to extract himself from the table they were all wedged in. When the small man was slow to exit the pub after their quarry, the Admiral hissed, 'Jump to it, man. We'll follow you with Pickles. He knows what you smell like...'

Willy Welbeck did indeed return to his boat shed, and as far as they could ascertain through the crack in the large rickety doors, he simply continued where he'd left off in the Red Lion.

'Now there's an unhappy man,' observed Jimmy sadly.

'Could be he's got something to hide,' muttered the Admiral. 'Murder can easily turn a man to drink'

'How would you know Charlie? Have you ever murdered anybody?' asked Mabel with a snort.

'Not recently,' Charles Shackleford muttered under his breath.

'Well that settles it, I'm definitely not about to go sailing with a drunkard.' Emily folded her arms decisively.

'Didn't stop you on that booze cruise last Christmas,' observed Jimmy mildly. 'I remember you saying how the boat rocking made you...'

'...That was different,' cut in Emily hastily, her face unaccountably pink in the fading light.

Both the Admiral and Mabel regarded Emily with renewed interest until a noise inside reminded them why they were there.

'It looks as though he's shutting up shop,' mumbled the Admiral. 'It's now or never Jimmy lad.'

Without warning, Charles Shackleford banged on the doors causing Willy to stop whatever he was doing and look up with a frown. After a second he headed towards the back, clearly intending to ignore whoever was at the door. Hastily the

Admiral hammered on the wood again causing Pickles to bark enthusiastically, until finally Willy hesitated, then turned back with a sigh and made his way towards them.

As he undid the bolt, all four sleuths stood back. 'Remember, we're tourists,' hissed the Admiral as their quarry pulled open the rickety door.

'Yes?' he asked curtly, eying them in suspiciously.

Jimmy stepped forward with a reassuring smile. 'We were told at the Red Lion you offer boat trips?'

Willy relaxed almost imperceptibly and stepped into the open doorway. 'Not much call for them this time o' year,' he repeated their earlier informant's observation.

Jimmy nodded and waved towards the now lowering sun behind them. 'I can understand that, but the weather's been lovely for the last few days and we all thought how wonderful it would be to see the glorious scenery from out in the bay.' Jimmy ended with a broad smile. Personally, the Admiral thought he was overdoing the gushing a bit, but their man certainly seemed to be weakening.

'We're only here until the day before Christmas Eve,' offered Mabel in an effort to close the deal.

'Well… I don't know. It depends on the weather. Forecast is good tomorrow.' It was clear the boat owner was tempted.

'Tomorrow?' squeaked Emily, 'We err…'

'…can pay you cash,' Jimmy interrupted, letting the comment sink in. Looking at the man's tattered clothing, it was a good bet Willy Welbeck needed the money.

'Fifty quid then. Cash. Upfront.' Emily narrowed her eyes and the Admiral stepped forward hurriedly before she had chance to put a spanner in the works. 'Done,' he announced enthusiastically. 'What time do you want us?'

'I'll meet you down at the harbour at eleven.' The door started to close in their face.

'ERR, WHAT'S THE NAME OF YOUR BOAT,' shouted Jimmy through the ever-narrowing crack.

'THE CODFATHER,' Willy shouted back before the door finally

slammed.

All four stared back at the door. Both the Admiral and Jimmy had the satisfied look of a job well done. Emily on the other hand was clearly spitting feathers. Mabel's thoughtful frown indicated she was very likely back with the possibility of a takeaway steak dinner.

'So, our suspect has a sense of humour,' observed Jimmy as they began to retrace their steps.

'Not something you'd expect a murderer to have,' added the Admiral, seemingly disappointed.

'We don't know he's a murderer Sir,' insisted Jimmy. 'Remember, the law states innocent until proven guilty.'

'I know, I know,' muttered the Admiral with an irritable sigh, 'but you've got to admit it would be bloody convenient.'

'What's not bloody convenient is a bloody boat trip tomorrow. I can tell you right now Jim Noon, I'm staying in the bloody lighthouse.' Emily quivered with outraged anger as she marched off in front.

'Glad I'm not in your shoes Jimmy lad,' said the Admiral with a wince. 'Going to cost you that is...'

Ten minutes later they were in front of the Red Lion. The Admiral looked down at his watch, wondering if they had time for another pint before it got dark.

'How are we going to get back to the lighthouse?' asked Mabel suddenly. Silence.

'I can't walk back Charlie,' continued Mabel, her mutinous expression warning the Admiral not to argue.

'It'll be dark soon anyway,' said Jimmy shaking his head, 'so walking's out of the question.' He turned towards the Admiral who for once looked stumped. 'Clearly we've been derelict in our duty Sir. Establishing our withdrawal strategy should have been our first priority on arrival.' The small man shook his head ruefully. 'I propose we investigate the possibility of public transport.'

The Admiral frowned. The prospect of a jerky bus journey along narrow roads in the dark was definitely not appealing - at the very least it would play havoc with his haemorrhoids.

'Might be worth looking up our mechanic friend,' he suggested. 'Mack said he intended to drive over to the lighthouse tonight to tell us the damage. If he was going to make the trip anyway, he might be up for giving us a lift.'

'Or the car might be fixed,' said Mabel hopefully.

'We could be wandering about for hours and it'll be dark soon,' reasoned Emily. 'We've got no idea where his garage is, and we've been all over the village.'

To her surprise, the Admiral nodded in agreement. 'You're spot on Emily. We'll pop back into the Red Lion and ask.' Without waiting to see if the others agreed, he turned and enthusiastically made his way towards the pub in front of them.

The warmth of the bar was welcome after the increasing cold outside and they elected to sit by the fire, a move Pickles wholeheartedly approved of. With a sigh, the elderly springer stretched out in front of the flames and closed his eyes.

The Admiral and Jimmy quickly made their way to the bar, returning a few minutes later with a couple of pints, two Proseccos and a pickled egg each to keep up moral. Enjoying the warmth as much as Pickles, the four of them sat in silence for a minute. The pub was almost empty after the afternoon rush, having yet to fill up for early evening.

'I spotted a notice board outside the ladies,' Emily commented at length. 'There were some cards advertising local builders and suchlike. I didn't pay much attention, but I remember noticing a drawing of a pickup truck on one of the cards. It could be our Mack.

'Good thinking Emily, I'll go and take a shufti,' said Jimmy climbing to his feet. He patted Emily on the shoulder as he squeezed past. 'We'll make a private investigator of you yet old girl.'

Five minutes later he was back, full of excitement. 'It's our Mack alright,' he said, sitting himself down, and what's more, he assured me the car will be fixed by tomorrow.'

'That doesn't solve tonight's bloody problem though does it,' the Admiral responded gloomily still concerned about his haemorrhoids.

'Well Sir, you'll be happy to know that he's also offered us a lift back to the lighthouse. For free.'

The Admiral's demeanour changed completely. 'Excellent work Jimmy lad,' he said, patting his subordinate on the back. 'I don't mind admitting I wasn't looking forward to the public transport option. When's he coming? Have we got time for another pint?'

'Ah, well, that's the *slight* fly in the ointment Sir,' Jimmy responded, causing the Admiral to pause in finishing his drink and regard the smaller man with narrowed eyes.

Jimmy took a deep breath. 'There's a carol service for the local school in the village hall. He's got to go there first to see his granddaughter in the choir.'

The Admiral gave a relieved sigh. 'That's not a problem Jimmy. We're warm and cosy, so we can just sit here until he fetches us. Might even treat ourselves to a nice steak while we're waiting.' The last was directed at Mabel who nodded happily.

Jimmy winced and coughed. 'The thing is Sir, I think he wants us to go along and support it...'

Chapter Five

The Admiral had never seen so many ankle biters in one place and the noise was deafening.

'What a cake and arse party,' he muttered to himself, looking around.

The whole affair reminded him uncomfortably of future stints of duty with his grandson Isaac. Fortunately, his own ankle biter was still in nappies and would not be requiring paper wings or a tinsel halo any time soon.

The truth was Charles Shackleford actually doted on his grandson and was very much afraid he might fall woefully short of the mark as a grandfather when the time came for him to do more than just bounce Isaac up and down on his knee.

Sighing, he turned his attention back to the present mayhem. The concert was being held in the village hall which appeared to have been decorated within an inch of its life. There was a huge Christmas tree in one corner draped with what must have been enough lights to power half the village and every available flat surface was festooned with paper garlands, no doubt made by the school children if the slapdash decorating was any clue. Thankfully the four of them had been directed to a row near the back where Pickles had promptly curled up into a ball underneath his master's chair.

The Admiral glanced around at his three companions, completely baffled as to why they actually seemed to be enjoying the ear-splitting pandemonium surrounding them. Children were running in and out of the hall and crawling under the rows of chairs. Some were yelling and shouting but most seemed to be snivelling for one reason or another. He sighed and looked at his watch, regretting the pickled egg now sitting like a lump of lead in his stomach.

Suddenly he felt a tug at his sleeve and looked down to see a small freckled face with a bright mop of ginger hair. The rug rat was dressed in what appeared to be a large white sheet and had a crown of tinsel resting drunkenly over one ear. To the Admiral's distaste, the aspiring angel also had a runny nose which he was currently enthusiastically licking at with his tongue. Resisting the urge to run for the hills, the Admiral made a concerted effort to plaster a smile on his face while he poked Mabel to get her attention.

Unfortunately, Mabel was in the middle of being educated by a woman seated in front of her on a ground-breaking technique for stuffing a turkey and was not responding to his increasingly urgent prods. Charles Shackleford was almost on the verge of offering his own creative elucidation of what exactly the woman in front could do with her bird, when a large man suddenly loomed at his side. From the matching shock of ginger hair, the Admiral surmised that the snotty rug rat was his son.

Breathing a sigh of relief, that he wasn't going to have to deal with the ankle biter after all, the Admiral prepared to turn away, but pulled up short when the stranger addressed him directly.

'So, I hear you're taking a boat trip tomorrow.' The Admiral looked up at him in surprise. 'Blimey, that was quick. We only booked it a couple of hours ago.' The man laughed and stuck out his hand.

'Name's John Dewer, and I only know about it because I'm coming with you. Willy called me after you left the shed.' The Admiral frowned. This put the cat amongst the pigeons and no mistake. How the bloody hell were they going to question Willy with the ginger nut tagging along?

'Does the boat need more than one crew member then?' asked Jimmy who'd clearly come to the same conclusion listening in.

John Dewer shook his head sombrely. 'Under normal

circumstances, no. But Willy's not been well, and this is the first time he's taken the Codfather out since the summer. Better to be safe than sorry, as they say.'

'Is the boat even seaworthy?' butted in Emily. The Admiral glanced at her irritably.

Their new friend was nodding his head. 'It's perfectly sound,' he offered reassuringly. 'Willy doesn't quite have the strength he once had, that's all, and thinks it would be better to have the two of us looking after you.'

'What's been wrong with him?' asked Mabel who'd clearly tired of learning about state-of-the-art turkey stuffing.

Their prospective first mate didn't answer immediately, being occupied with wiping his son's nose. When he finally straightened, he looked sad. "Lost his daughter less than a month ago. She took her own life.'

'I thought she was his...' the Admiral started to say

'...That's a terrible thing to happen. And just before Christmas too,' interrupted Jimmy hastily. 'I can see how the man must be heartbroken.'

'Are you sure he should be taking us out on the boat tomorrow?' asked Emily hopefully

'It'll do him good,' John responded. 'Willy needs something to take his mind off what happened...' He paused abruptly, and they almost missed his next whispered words, 'As do I.'

'What exactly did happen?' the Admiral managed to finish his sentence this time after glaring at Jimmy.

John Dewer blinked and sighed, making an obvious effort to shake off his melancholy. 'The inquest said it was depression. Jenny's mum upped and left a few years ago leaving both her and Willy devastated. Christmas is always the time when we miss absent family the most, I suppose.'

The Admiral tried to avoid looking at the rug rat directly in his eye line who was now busy picking his nose.

'Stop that Archie,' John admonished, adjusting his son's lopsided halo. His mini me responded by holding up a large bogey for his father's inspection. The Admiral swallowed, wondering if his pickled egg was likely to make an appearance. Expertly wiping the offending digit, their informant continued.

'Jenny was the cleaner at Whitebeam lighthouse up the coast - it's used as a holiday let. She was getting the place ready when for some reason it all got too much for her. She left a note saying she couldn't live without her mum anymore and threw herself off the top of the lighthouse.' He paused again and shook his head. 'Her body was found on the doorstep the next morning.'

'Must have been a terrible shock,' murmured Mabel with a shudder. 'Who found her exactly?'

'It was a couple,' John answered, confirming Mack's earlier story. 'I think they'd just come over to Morwelly for a short break.' He grimaced. 'Not exactly a good start to anybody's holiday.'

'I should think not,' agreed Mabel with a small shudder. 'I wouldn't have fancied staying at the lighthouse after seeing that.'

John nodded. 'I don't think they did either. Apparently, they booked into a bed and breakfast in the village for the few days while they waited for the police enquiry to be over.'

'Were they from up country?' asked the Admiral, trying his best to sound nonchalant.

There was another pause before their informant answered. 'I'm not sure, I seem to remember they told Connie they live over on Dartmoor.'

'Who's Connie?' asked Emily.

'Connie Baxter,' John clarified. 'She owns the Beach House bed and breakfast. The pair stayed with her for about three days I think it was.'

'Strange they didn't go straight home really,' mused Jimmy. 'The police could easily have visited them at their house.'

Their informant shrugged dismissively. 'The weather can be pretty bleak up there in the winter. No doubt they thought to enjoy the milder climate of the coast for a bit longer.'

'Why did Jenny's mum up and leave in the first place?' the Admiral asked.

John shook his head, seemingly unsurprised about the question. 'Why does any couple split up? I don't think Willy and Deborah were getting along.'

'But to leave her daughter?' Emily questioned shaking her head. 'Not many women would do that.'

John shrugged again, this time looking uncomfortable. 'Nobody knows why she left. Jenny was a teenager and you know what young people are like. They didn't...'

Unfortunately, the rest of his reply was lost as a loud clapping sounded from the front of the hall.

'Ladies and gentlemen, we are now ready to begin our Christmas concert, so could you please return to your seats.'

John Dewer bent to pick up his son. 'It was very nice meeting you all,' he said hastily, 'Please don't have any concerns about your boat trip. Willy and I are both very experienced sailors. We'll make sure you all have a wonderful day tomorrow.' Before the Admiral had chance to say anything further, he disappeared into the throng.

'Bollocks,' Charles Shackleford muttered with a sigh.

'There might be some time at the end to find out a bit more,' shouted Jimmy over the din as the school choir assembled on the stage. It had to be said that most of the assembling seemed to consist of shoving, pushing and kicking, and the Admiral frowned in disapproval. At this rate they were likely to witness another murder before they even launched into the first Christmas carol.

'They all need a bloody good stint in uniform,' he muttered darkly. 'That would whip 'em into shape.'

'There's not one of them over ten,' responded Jimmy shaking his head, 'I don't think shaving their heads and making them march twenty miles over barren and hostile territory is going to give the right kind of guidance at this stage in their lives.'

'Well it certainly wouldn't do that little bugger any harm,' retorted the Admiral pointing at a boy currently spraying glitter up the nose of his classmate.

Finally, the choir launched into *Hark the Herald Angels Sing* and Charles Shackleford slumped down in his chair with a sigh and turned his mind towards their investigation. As much as he was loath to admit it, their attendance at the concert might just give them the edge they needed to crack the case. He looked around, wondering whether Connie Baxter was in the audience. There was a good chance she was here somewhere. He made a note to look for the Beach House owner after the bloody awful racket was over...

The Admiral lasted three quarters of an hour before he dropped off, only to be abruptly awakened by a totally unprovoked poke in the ribs from Mabel ten minutes later. She glared at him before remarking to Emily that it was beyond her how anyone could possibly sleep through such a fervent interpretation of *Oh Come All Ye Faithful*. Emily agreed wholeheartedly. Jimmy looked pained, and the object of her censure thought he'd better pull out his ear plugs.

Fortunately, the concert only lasted another half an hour after that, and both the Admiral and Jimmy, not to mention Pickles, were beyond relieved when they were invited for mulled wine and mince pies in the room next door.

'Keep an eye out for Connie Baxter,' the Admiral said to the other three as he picked up his third mince pie. 'I'd like to know if the couple who found the body had anything to say.'

'We could do with finding out their names as well,' added Jimmy hastily before Mabel had chance comment on her larger half's weakness for all things sweet.

'We should split up,' Emily suggested, 'that way we can cover more ground.'

'Good thinking,' the Admiral attempted to say round a mouth full of mince pie, promptly spraying sultanas and pastry crumbs everywhere - causing those in the immediate vicinity to step back hurriedly. The exception was Pickles who was delighted it appeared to be raining food.

'Charlie your manners are atrocious,' declared Mabel with a sniff before marching off to do her sleuthing elsewhere. Bemused, the Admiral watched her go. 'Sometimes there's just no pleasing women,' he complained to Jimmy before helping himself to mince pie number four.

Jimmy wisely refrained from commenting and elected to follow his wife - for two reasons that actually had nothing to do with his former commanding officer's eating habits.

Firstly, the Admiral's version of interrogation, especially at large gatherings, was at best embarrassing, and at worst likely to get them thrown out. Secondly, in his experience, women had a nose for gossip. It was something he'd learned the hard way after being married for so many years...

In the end though, it was Mabel who finally located the elusive Ms Connie Baxter, already on her fifth glass of mulled wine and clearly the worse for wear. She was a small bird of a woman with a loud screeching laugh that reminded Mabel of a rusty nail scraping down a blackboard.

'So, you're not a local,' observed Connie after the initial introductions had been made.

'We're from South Devon,' trilled Mabel, trying to look over her companion's head for the other three. 'I won a competition for a five-day mini break in Whitebeam lighthouse,' she finished proudly. Unfortunately, her announcement concerning their accommodation came at the same time as her newfound friend was taking a slurp of her mulled wine and most of it ended up decorating the front of Mabel's best jumper.

'God, I'm so sorry,' mumbled Connie, trying to mop down the front of Mabel's sweater and merely succeeding in sloshing the rest of the wine over the floor. Backing off hurriedly, Mabel rummaged around her handbag, finally discovering an ancient tissue which she dabbed futilely at the splashes. 'Please don't worry,' she murmured, 'I'm sure it will come out in the wash.' They subsided into silence while Connie topped up her now empty glass and Mabel tried vainly to locate the other three before her quarry did a runner. She was so busy craning her neck and throwing her arm up in the air every time she thought she caught a glimpse, that her companion eventually frowned and questioned with concern as to whether she'd been tested for Tourette's.

Mabel had finally located the others and was now maniacally waving her hand in the air. Finally turning back to look at her companion, she said, 'It wasn't really a test, I just had to answer three questions. I don't think it mattered whether I was a tourist or not,' she gave a beaming smile, just as Jimmy and Emily appeared at her shoulder.

'This is Connie,' Mabel said waving at her bemused acquaintance.

'What on earth have you done to your sweater?' asked Emily, staring at the red stains decorating Mabel's front. 'Have you had one too many glasses of mulled wine Mabel?'

'No that would be me,' Connie screeched with laughter, waving her glass around as proof. Both Jimmy and Emily automatically recoiled at the horrendous noise before smiling politely, all the time wondering how best to bring up the delicate subject of a dead body being discovered by two of her guests. Jimmy was just about to speak when Mabel managed to get in first.

'I was telling Connie that we're staying at Whitebeam lighthouse and I think she was a little surprised.' She turned back to their quarry. 'Was it because of that girl throwing herself out of the window Connie?'

Jimmy winced, seriously concerned that the Admiral's lack of tact was beginning to rub off on Mabel.

'Bloody hell, what was that noise,' asked the subject of his thoughts, suddenly materialising with Pickles in tow. 'Sounded like a strangled parrot.'

Jimmy sighed, unexpectedly longing for the days when he was the ship's Master at Arms and in charge of any onboard investigation. Things were rapidly getting out of hand.

Before the Admiral could put in his two pennies worth, Jimmy hurriedly stepped in.

'We were all extremely sorry to hear about the tragedy at the lighthouse Ms Baxter. Obviously, we weren't aware of it before we arrived. Was the young girl a friend of yours?'

Connie Baxter shook her head gravely, clearly struggling to remember who they were actually talking about.

'Any minute now they're going to be carrying her out,' mumbled the Admiral impatiently. 'Get on with it Jimmy.'

'I understand the couple who found her stayed at your bed and breakfast,' the small man continued.

'The Beach House,' offered Mabel helpfully in case their drunken friend happened to forget the name of her home.

Connie shook her head, this time woefully, before taking another drink and wobbling ominously.

'She said it would haunt her for the rest of her days. I said Iris darling, you mustn't dwell on it. She…'

'Iris what?' interrupted the Admiral aiming to get as much intelligence as possible before their informant fell over.

Connie blinked at him and frowned.

'What was the couple's surname?' clarified Emily.

There a pause and they all waited with bated breath.

'Denmead,' she announced triumphantly after what seemed like an age. 'Their names were Jim and Iris Denmead.' Then in slow motion, Connie Baxter toppled forward, only saved at the last second by Jimmy's quick action. Instead of the floor, their informant fell into the small man's arms. She looked up at her rescuer adding, 'She was born here you know.'

Chapter Eleven

Squashing into Mack's old truck proved as challenging as the first time they'd experienced it.

The problem was, on this occasion there were the additional, not to mention explosive, complications of pickled eggs, mince pies, beer and mulled wine.

Mabel appeared to have abandoned her earlier request for a takeaway steak dinner, declaring weakly that she believed she'd eaten enough.

After that, nobody actually spoke at all, even when the elderly mechanic put his foot down along the coast road leading to the lighthouse, arriving in a record breaking ten minutes and twenty seconds.

The very real possibility of asphyxiation was clearly uppermost in all of the truck's occupants and as soon as the vehicle skidded to a stop with a squeal of brakes and smell of burning rubber impressive enough to rival anything out of a *Fast and Furious* movie, they all fell over each other to climb out as quickly as possible. Including Pickles.

Once back in the fresh air, both Mabel and Emily glared at the Admiral before thanking Mack politely for bringing them back. The mechanic didn't answer immediately, being understandably focused on getting some breathable air into his lungs. His colour was an interesting shade of green, and the alternating light and shadow cast by the lighthouse lantern left him bearing more than a passing resemblance to the creature from the black lagoon.

At the very least Jimmy feared the whole experience might well add a few pounds to their repair bill.

Eventually Mac straightened and coughed before rasping out that he'd bring the car over early in the morning along with their invoice. Climbing cautiously back into his truck, he slammed the door and started the engine, only to lean his head out of the hastily wound down window to recommend they stay off the pickled eggs served at the Red Lion. Apparently, the hors d'oeuvres were well known in local circles for being lethal. And with that sage advice he disappeared off into the dark.

The Admiral was uncharacteristically sheepish as he unlocked the door, even allowing the three of them to precede him out of the cold. In fact, for a few seconds Jimmy actually thought he was going to apologise, but the moment passed...

Conserving their energy for the climb up the steep stairs, all four remained silent, the only noise coming from Pickles dancing around eagerly at the top, obviously ready for his dinner. On reaching the cosy sitting room, they collapsed breathlessly onto the comfortable sofas. Jimmy was the first one to recover, mostly because Pickles was climbing all over him - no doubt in the belief that his master's best friend was the one most likely to feed him. Sighing, Jimmy pushed the enthusiastic dog onto the floor. Then, reasoning that their journey back to the lighthouse was clearly a low point in their trip and best forgotten, asked if anyone would like a cup of tea...

Fortified with some chocolate hobnobs which seemed to do the trick with regards to the pickled eggs, the Admiral recovered his usual aplomb

'Right then, what now?'

'I think a visit to your doctor might be wise,' offered Emily with pursed lips, still not ready to forgive their earlier embarrassment.

Ever the peacemaker, Jimmy hastily jumped in. 'It would be helpful if we could question the Denmeads, but as of yet we don't have an address and we can't just go wondering around Dartmoor in the few days we have left.'

'And the boat trip might well end up being a washout with the ginger nut on board,' added the Admiral gloomily.

'We'll just have to get there early Sir,' responded Jimmy. 'Mack said he would bring the car over first thing, so we should be able to get into the village well before our sailing time. Hopefully we'll arrive before John Dewer does and have a chance to give Willy a bit of a grilling on his own. He paused for a moment. 'First thing's first though. As soon as it's light, we need to take a look in the lantern tower. Like I said earlier, there might be some evidence the police missed. Especially if they weren't looking for a murderer.'

All four of them glanced towards the shadowy stairs with less than their customary enthusiasm, then the Admiral sighed. 'Best get an early night then,' he said polishing off the last hobnob.

Luckily for all of them except Emily, the next day dawned bright and sunny. More tea with buttered toast and marmalade went a long way to restoring enthusiasm and by quarter to eight, they were clustered around the bottom of the stairs. Needless to say, Pickles didn't move from in front of the fire.

'Right then,' stated the Admiral in a voice that brooked no nonsense. 'We'll take it in stages. I want us all to muster in the lantern tower by Oh eight hundred and not a minute later. First leg is up to mine and Mabel's room.' With that, he determinedly made a start, leaving the others to follow in single file behind him.

In the event, it took them almost thirty minutes to do the climb and by the time they reached the top, even Jimmy was in the throes of a galloping comeback. Fortunately, a circular wooden bench fixed to the wall provided an emergency resting place and they spent the next ten minutes waiting for heart rates to go down and blood pressures to settle.

'If I have to do that again, I'll be joining Davy Jones in his bloody locker,' wheezed the Admiral eventually.

'Amen,' muttered Emily under her breath.

On this occasion, it was actually Mabel who recovered first and her amazement as she took her first glimpse of the incredible three-hundred-and-sixty-degree view out of the window got the other three to their feet.

'You can actually see Dartmoor from here,' exclaimed Jimmy pointing inland.

'And I reckon that might be the Gower Peninsula and over there is Lundy Island,' offered the Admiral.

'It's nice to see you haven't lost your irrigational skills Charlie,' enthused Mabel

'It's navigational skills,' responded Emily tetchily, and he's just reading that map on the wall.' She sniffed before continuing 'I'd be surprised if he ever had any navigational abilities. I certainly wouldn't be getting on that boat today if Charlie was the skipper.'

'You wouldn't have been bloody invited if I was the skipper,' bristled the Admiral.

'Enough,' barked Jimmy, glaring at them. 'It's like listening to a couple of children bickering and quarrelling. Any more arguing and I'll be forced to take further action.'

Both the Admiral and Emily turned to Jimmy in surprise. Charles Shackleford opened his mouth to reply, but for once in his life had no response. Emily went pink and looked at her husband with renewed interest.

'Right then,' Jimmy continued in a milder tone. 'We're here for a purpose. None of us is going to want to make this climb again, so it's vital we give the place a damn good once over to see if we can find any clues the plod might have missed.'

The Admiral nodded, only just resisting the urge to salute. His old friend was always a bloody good Master at Arms.

The next ten minutes were significantly quieter as they each began examining a different area of the circular room. 'There's nothing here,' the Admiral muttered at length. 'We're going to have to go outside and have a shufti at where she actually jumped from.'

Both ladies looked at the narrow balcony circling the outside of the tower with a shudder. At this height, the wind was howling.

'It's blowing a bloody hooley out there,' added the Admiral, vocalising their thoughts, 'so it's likely any evidence will have long since blown away.'

'Nevertheless, we need to take a look,' Jimmy countered, still in his best Master at Arms voice. He turned to Emily and Mabel. 'You ladies stay here in the warmth. Sir, you come with me.' Then without further ado, he turned and grasped the handle of the outside door, and taking a deep breath, pulled it open.

A gust of wind blew the door the rest of the way. 'Be careful Jim,' called Emily suddenly fearing her husband might be the next casualty of their investigation.

Charles Shackleford reluctantly followed the small man out into the swirling wind and together they pulled the door shut behind them.

'We'll go in opposite directions, cross over on the other side and meet back here,' Jimmy shouted. The Admiral offered a thumbs up and they turned to examining the railing, slowly working their way around the narrow walkway.

An entire circuit failed to produce anything of note and the Admiral was all for calling it a day, but suddenly he spotted something out of the corner of his eye caught underneath the corner of the door, in between the door panel and the frame. Frowning, he tapped Jimmy's shoulder and pointed. The small man got down on his hands and knees to get a closer look at what appeared to be a small scrap of cloth. Pulling a clean tissue from his pocket, he grasped the very edge and pulled, but the piece was firmly stuck. Without taking his eyes off the tiny prize, he yelled at the Admiral to open the door as slowly as he could. However, the wind had other ideas, and as soon as Charles Shackleford grasped the handle, the door flew inwards out of his hands.

Luckily, the fragment remained firmly wedged but now Jimmy was finally able to pull it free. Triumphant, both men hurried back into the sunny warmth of the tower to examine their discovery.

Clustering round, all four stared down at their find. 'It looks like it might be from a coat,' Emily observed. 'That looks like a bit of velcro underneath. Turn it over Jimmy.'

Turning the scrap over, they spied what did indeed look to be the very edge of some kind of velcro fastening.

And stuck firmly to it was a long, bright ginger hair.

In contrast to their ascent, coming down the stairs proved quicker, if not easier. Or it would have been had they all not decided to pay a visit to their respective ensuite facilities on route.

When they finally reconvened in the sitting room, Mabel complained of pins and needles in both legs and Emily was nursing her bunion. 'I'm really not sure I'm up to a boat trip after the exercise we've already had this morning,' Mabel murmured as she rubbed at her aching calves. Emily nodded her head in agreement, relieved to finally have some support.

The Admiral tutted irritably at the very idea of cancelling, while secretly hoping Jimmy would agree it was all too much. Instead the small man advised a fortifying tot of brandy to go with their coffee. 'That'll get you back on your feet in no time ladies,' he advised, handing each of them a snifter.

'I'm afraid the trip is even more important now we know that someone with red hair may have been on the lantern balcony. John Dewer might well be a suspect.'

'But why on earth would he want to push his friend's stepdaughter to her death?' asked Emily, still reluctant to take to the water. 'I mean he seemed really upset last night over what had happened to Jenny.'

'That's what we need to find out,' advised Jimmy firmly. 'Right now, John's only connection appears to be his acquaintance with Willy and his obvious sadness over the stepdaughter's death. But what if there's something we're missing?'

'Could he have been having an affair with Willy's missis?' the Admiral asked, forgetting about his aches and pains.

'Why would he murder Jenny then?'

'He might have murdered her mother and Jenny found out.' The Admiral's voice was excited now, 'Or he might have been having an affair with Jenny herself!'

'Before we get carried away,' Jimmy interrupted with the voice of reason, 'the ginger hair could belong to anybody and it certainly doesn't mean John Dewer was in the lantern tower at the time Jenny died. That's why we need to talk to him.' He looked over at the Admiral. 'Please don't take this the wrong way Sir, but it's very important that we're circumspect in our questioning. We can't afford to accuse him of anything or, if he does turn out to be guilty, show our hand too early.' Charles Shackleford frowned, but before he had time to answer, Jimmy turned to Emily and Mabel.

'Instead of coming with us on the boat today, why don't you both pay a visit to the Beach House and see if you can get anything else useful from Connie Baxter? She might well have the Denmeads' address.' Both Mabel and Emily looked at each other and nodded with relief

The Admiral was just about to take another sip of his brandy when a horn sounded outside

'You be careful how much you drink Charlie,' Mabel cautioned her other half, 'I'm not stepping foot in that car if you have more than a couple of sips.'

The Admiral sighed and put the glass down while Jimmy waved at the mechanic through one of the narrow windows. Mack waved the keys along with an envelope back at him before pushing them underneath the lighthouse door.

'I don't think he's waiting for us to give him a lift back into town,' commented Mabel as she watched the mechanic climb into a second car.

'Well can you blame him?' responded Emily caustically.

Ten minutes later they were climbing into the car which smelled rather strongly of pine air freshener courtesy of a dangly cardboard tree hanging from the rear-view mirror. Clearly Mack had thought to pre-empt any further breathing difficulties resulting from the previous evening's overindulgence of hors d'oeuvres.

That was all well and good but the scent of pine permeating the car was so strong that by the time they'd parked up and got out, Mabel complained that she smelled like a public lavatory.

Thinking silence on this occasion was the best option, Jimmy hurried round to open the boot and grab the rest of their sailing gear. Both veterans of the sea, albeit from many years ago, the

Admiral and Jimmy pulled on boots and waterproof sailing jackets that looked as though they'd last been worn during the seventies - which was quite probable. Wrinkling her nose and deciding that smelling like a toilet was actually better than a sweaty sailor, Mabel hurriedly stepped away to pull on her own faux fur.

'Right then, let's synchronise watches,' the Admiral ordered once they were all suitably dressed. 'Me and Jimmy'll head straight over to the harbour with Pickles. We've got an hour before we're due to sail so with a bit of luck we'll collar old Willy while he's on his own. Once we're on the boat, we can turn our attention to the ginger nut. Divide and conquer so to speak.' Jimmy winced but didn't offer any objections.

'What's your plan ladies?' he asked Mabel and Emily instead.

'It's still a bit early to go knocking on Connie Baxter's door, so I think it would be best if we start by having another coffee at that nice tea rooms we went in yesterday,' Emily reasoned. 'What do you think Mabel?'

'Ooh yes, another piece of that lovely Christmas cake would go down a treat.' Mabel thought for a second before adding, 'And we might get a chance for another little chat with that young girl who knew Jenny.'

'Right then,' the Admiral repeated, 'We're unlikely to be more than a couple of hours afloat so I say we muster back here at thirteen fifteen hours and go for a quick pint in the Red Lion to share intel. What do you think Jimmy?' Surprised at actually being consulted, the small man nodded without speaking, and shortly after, they separated.

Chapter Twelve

The Admiral and Jimmy took their time walking down to the harbour.

They still had forty-five minutes until they were officially due to meet Willy and they didn't want to arrive too early, preferring to surprise him once he was already on board.

The Admiral let Pickles off the lead as they walked down the picturesque cobbled street. There were very few cars that could fit down the narrow thoroughfare and the Admiral wasn't unduly worried at the prospect of the springer getting himself lost. As he proudly informed Jimmy, Pickles' nose could pick out his master's scent in the dark from a hundred yards away - even without the pickled eggs.

The street abruptly opened up into the quaint little harbour which was surrounded on one side by a protective sea wall and on the other by three very old fisherman's cottages which, judging by their chocolate box appearance were now used as holiday lettings. The tide was on its way in and they had no trouble identifying the Codfather out of the three vessels currently moored up.

'Let's try and have a bit of a shufti first without alerting old Willy,' the Admiral suggested as they approached the first of the three boats. 'If he's there yet,' responded Jimmy narrowing his eyes to squint in the sun. 'I can't see anyone onboard.' They came alongside the middle boat which appeared almost derelict. It also looked deserted, but as they walked past, Pickles suddenly stopped and began whining slightly. Pausing, the Admiral bent down to fuss the spaniel. 'What's wrong lad,' he murmured, just as the sound of raised voices came through a porthole.

'Sounds like Willy,' Jimmy said with a frown.

'Well whoever he's talking to, they don't sound very happy,' the Admiral commented, bending down to put Pickles back on his lead. The springer pulled slightly, then seemed to settle down.

The two men walked a little further so they were hidden from view behind the bow and listened intently as the voices got louder.

'I don't care what you say Willy, it was a stupid thing to do.'

'Sounds like a woman,' whispered Jimmy.

They missed Willy's reply, but it was easy to deduce when the woman continued, 'I know you need the money, but I'm telling you they're interested in more than a damn boat trip. They're strangers here. Seriously, why would four geriatrics come to stay in Whitebeam lighthouse of all places five days before Christmas and ask to go on a spur-of-the-moment pleasure cruise on your boat? It doesn't add up.'

'Bloody cheek,' muttered the Admiral, 'She makes it sound as if we've got one foot in the bollocking grave.' Jimmy held up his hand and the large man subsided.

'They've been asking questions about Jenny,' the woman hissed.

'Jenny committed suicide,' Willy's response was a near shout. 'She killed herself. Threw herself off the top of a lighthouse. How clear is that?'

'But they wanted to know why she did it Willy.' The woman's voice was patient, as though talking to a child. It was clear she was trying to calm her companion down. Instead, her soothing tone seemed to have the opposite effect. 'I don't know why she bloody well killed herself,' Willy cried out, the anguish in his voice clearly unfeigned. 'I thought she'd be happy.' They heard muffled weeping and looked silently at each other.

'We need to see who he's talking to,' Jimmy whispered. They waited for another couple of minutes as the broken man's weeping slowly subsided, even the Admiral felt like a grubby rubberneck being witness to Willy's pain.

Eventually the woman spoke in a tired voice. 'It wasn't your fault Willy. 'You couldn't have known what effect the news would have on her.'

'If I had, I'd have kept it to myself,' sniffed Willy. 'I might have thought Jenny was a spoilt brat, but I didn't want her to die.'

'I know you didn't,' the woman soothed, 'Everybody knows it wasn't your fault. You've got to stop blaming yourself Willy. And drinking yourself to death isn't the answer either. We'll get through this. We just don't want outsiders coming in and snooping around.' Willy didn't answer and his companion continued, her voice sharper now. 'Cancel the trip Willy. When they get here, tell them there's a problem with the boat. I've spoken to John already so if they bump into him before they leave, he'll back up your story. They'll be gone in another three days and we can all relax. Anyway, I have to go.' There was a rustling followed by the sound of footsteps coming up onto the deck.

The Admiral and Jimmy instinctively shrank back, pulling Pickles with them, knowing that if the woman chose to walk in the direction of the Codfather, they'd be rumbled. Holding their breaths, they watched her walk carefully down the gangplank onto the safety of the quay where luckily for them she turned to walk the other way. Not so luckily it also meant they didn't get a good look at her. 'Turn round,' mumbled the Admiral, willing the woman to look back.

'What time are you coming over tomorrow tonight?' Willy's sudden appearance on the deck caught them by surprise, but it had the desired result as the woman stop and turned. Unfortunately, neither the Admiral nor Jimmy had ever seen her before.

'I want to get the whole thing over with,' Willy continued, 'once and for all. I can't deal with it any longer.'

The woman didn't answer for a second, then she nodded sharply. 'We'll be there at nine,' she said in a clipped tone before swinging back round and walking quickly away.

Jimmy and the Admiral continued to huddle on the port side of the bow unsure whether to make a run for it, but if they moved now, Willy would know they'd been privy to his conversation. Again, the gods were smiling on them because, after a loud sigh,

Willy turned and went back down into the cabin.

∞∞∞

Mabel and Emily were enjoying the peace and quiet without their noisier other halves. Or rather, one half of their other halves. The tea rooms were busy but not unpleasantly so and there was a nicely festive atmosphere with the waitresses dressed as elves and fairies. They'd elected this time to share the enormous piece of Christmas cake and in a particularly decadent move in Mabel's opinion, Emily had requested it be served with a large dollop of brandy cream.

Their waitress on this occasion was a very friendly, rather large lady whose elf costume was in grave danger of turning into a green and red swimsuit. There was no sign of their waitress from the day before which was disappointing as they'd hope to glean a little more information about Jenny Welbeck's state of mind. However, as Emily remarked, it was actually rather nice to relax and enjoy their cake and simply chat without having to keep abreast of the latest interrogation tactics.

'It's certainly very popular in here,' Mabel observed as the last table was taken. 'I wouldn't mind giving their fish and chips a go if we get the chance.'

Emily nodded her head in agreement. 'I'll ask if they do a special offer for pensioners,' she stated, putting up her hand to catch their waitress's attention. Sadly, their particular attendant was now busy serving the newly arrived customers and, after acknowledging their appeal with a quick smile, she waved another member of staff towards their table. The cheerful young man heading towards them was unexpectedly dressed as the sugar plum fairy, and the effusive way he greeted them indicated a strong possibility that he batted for the other side.

'Good morning,' he enthused clapping his hands, 'What can I do for you lovely ladies today?' Emily smiled back at him, thanking her lucky stars that the Admiral was not with them on this occasion. While Charlie was not particularly discriminatory towards gay people - at least no more than he discriminated against anyone else - his lack of diplomacy had led Emily to accuse him on more than one occasion of being 'as subtle as a brick.'

'Do you serve a special pensioner's portion of fish and chips?' she asked.

'*No...* You gorgeous girls can't possibly be pensioners,' their waiter exclaimed shaking his head and covering his mouth up in mock disbelief.

Neither Mabel or Emily were immune to flattery no matter what side of the fence it came from, and they both giggled almost simultaneously. 'I'm over seventy,' added Mabel proudly. The young man, whose name badge said he was called Kevin, put his hand on his hip and whistled under his breath. 'I never would have believed it my darling. Not in a million years. You don't look a day older than my mum.' He waved his hand towards the other side of the tearoom giving them a good idea that his mother might well be the owner of the establishment.

'We saw a very nice young lady yesterday,' said Emily thinking they really ought to get a bit of sleuthing in if at all possible. 'She sounded very sad. I think she'd lost a friend recently. I couldn't help but notice that she's not here today. I really hope she's alright.'

Kevin tapped his pen thoughtfully against his beautifully painted plum lips. 'Oh, you mean Karen,' he said eventually. Then he shook his head mournfully. 'They were absolute besties, it's so sad.' He leaned forward to continue in a low voice. 'Between me and you, my mum was completely cut up too when she heard what happened. She and Jenny's mum were like sisters until Debra upped and left with nary a word to anyone. Since then...'

'Kevin, I hope you're not wasting time in idle gossip.' The owner of the voice was a neatly dressed middle aged lady whose festive costume consisted solely of a sprig of holly attached to her apron. She spoke mildly but there was a slight underlying note of disapproval and Kevin hurriedly explained that these two lovely ladies had been asking about their pensioner's specials. The waitress smiled at him in affectionate exasperation before patting him on the arm. 'In that case dear, just pop and get a copy of the specials menu. That will give these ladies all the information they need.'

'Yes mum,' responded Kevin and after giving Mabel and Emily an apologetic smile, he hurried away.

'What a delightful son you have,' commented Mabel.

The woman sighed. 'My Kevin's a lovely boy but he'd rather stand around chatting than work. Pay no heed to his gossip.'

Emily glanced at Mabel and frowned slightly thinking what an odd thing to say. She was about to reply when she suddenly caught sight of her husband's face in the window. There was no sign of the Admiral. 'I wonder what Jimmy's doing back so soon?' she murmured to Mabel before turning back to their waitress who was staring out of the window at Jimmy with a strange look on her face.

'I'm afraid we have to go,' Emily apologised, 'Could we have the bill please?'

'I'll send it along with Kevin,' responded the waitress, gathering up their plates. As she leant forward, Emily managed to read the words on her badge. *Kathy Brummel, Proprietor.* 'The cake was lovely,' Mabel offered with a smile. 'We'll definitely be back.'

A couple of minutes later, Kevin arrived back at the table with the promised specials menu. 'Would you like to book a table?' he asked, 'To be honest we're pretty busy over the next few days being as it's nearly Christmas so it might be a good idea.'

Emily glanced out at Jimmy waiting impatiently in the cold. 'Do you have a card?' she asked standing to put on her coat. Kevin rummaged around in his apron pocket, proudly producing a small creased piece of paper. 'Here you go,' he said with a smile. 'Just ask for Kevin when you call.' He leaned forward conspiratorially. 'We get a bit extra for taking bookings.' Emily smiled back and slipped the card into her handbag. 'Thank you, Kevin, you've been very helpful,' she murmured as they turned towards the door.

'You're very welcome he called after them. 'I think Karen should be working over the next two days, so if you come again, you'll probably get to see her. Anyhow, I'll tell her you were asking after her.'

Emily waved in acknowledgement while speaking in an undertone to Mabel. 'I hope he doesn't mention it to that poor girl. Charlie didn't exactly leave a positive impression.'

'When does he ever?' snorted Mabel shaking her head.

A few seconds later they were outside, shivering at the sudden change in temperature. 'Where's Charlie?' asked Mabel looking around.

'I left him with Willy talking about things that can go wrong with boats,' Jimmy responded.

'Was that wise Jimmy?' frowned Emily, 'You're taking a huge risk leaving Charlie unsupervised, and anyway why aren't you both out experiencing life on the ocean wave again?'

'Sometimes plain-speaking is exactly what's needed,' returned Jimmy in defence of his oldest friend, 'and Willy cancelled us, supposedly because there's a mechanical problem with the boat.'

'But you don't think there is?'

Jimmy shook his head. 'Who was that woman you were speaking to at the table?'

'Her name's Kathy Brummel, she owns the tea rooms,' said Mabel. 'Why?'

'We overheard someone talking to Willy earlier,' said Jimmy. 'They didn't know we were listening. It was a woman, and she was hauling him over the coals about booking us on the boat trip.

'I wonder why?' questioned Emily. 'Did you manage to get a good look at her?'

Jimmy nodded then tipped his head back towards the busy tearoom. 'It was her, Kathy Brummel. She ordered Willy to cancel our trip.'

Chapter Fourteen

It was another ten minutes before they finally spotted the Admiral heading up the cobbled street towards them and by the time he caught up with them he was red faced and breathless.

Mabel eyed him with concern until eventually he pointed towards the Red Lion and managed to wheeze out the word, 'Pint.'

'It's only half past eleven,' said Mabel disapprovingly.

'Sun's over the yardarm somewhere in the world,' puffed the Admiral, 'and after the bloody exercise I've had this morning, they'll be lucky I don't ask for a straw.' He turned and staggered towards the pub, Pickles in tow without waiting to see if the others followed.

The inside was predictably cosy and warm and Emily and Mabel wasted no time in warming their hands by the roaring fire. 'I thought we were supposed to be questioning Connie Baxter,' said Mabel once they were all seated.

'I think it's more important we're all updated with recent events,' responded Jimmy. A lot seems to have happened this morning and I'm beginning to feel as though we're missing something vital.'

'We can still go and interrogate our landlady after we've finished here,' suggested the Admiral, clearly a little more the ticket after a few sips of his beer.

'What did Willy have to say for himself after I left?' Jimmy asked.

Charles Shackleford snorted. 'Very little. He didn't seem able to give any reason as to why the Codfather couldn't put to sea, and as a boat owner, he should be able to come up with a dozen convincing porkies. All very bloody strange. Any sailor should have a working knowledge of his vessel's mechanics at the very least and I got the impression Willy's a pretty old sea dog.' The Admiral frowned. 'It was like he'd just forgotten.'

'It might be stress or simple anxiety,' suggested Jimmy. 'He seemed pretty upset and anxious when he was talking to Kathy Brummel.'

'Kathy who?' the Admiral asked with a frown. Realising they were getting ahead of themselves; Jimmy took the next fifteen minutes to bring everybody up to speed with the morning's developments.

'So, there's clearly something fishy going on,' Jimmy finished, 'but the bottom line is we haven't got a bloody clue what.'

'And we've only got three more days to find out,' added Emily.

'Well, whatever happened to Jenny or her mother, it doesn't look as though Willy Welbeck is the cold hearted killer we thought him to be.'

'But we're obviously not the only ones who've been thinking it,' Jimmy murmured remembering their elderly mole of the day before, not to mention Mack's words when he first dropped them off.

'Well Jenny's friend Karen definitely thought he was capable of murder,' Emily said, adding to the list.

The Admiral sighed. 'I wonder if that old timer we spoke to yesterday will be in this lunchtime?'

'I'm not sure he'd have anything more useful to tell us anyway Sir,' Jimmy said.

'Bloody good job now I think about it, given how much it's cost me so far.'

'Let's just go over what we know,' Jimmy suggested, taking a deep breath.

'Jenny Welbeck was killed either by her own hand or somebody else's nearly two weeks ago now leaving a note saying she couldn't stand being without her mother any longer - or something along those lines anyway.

'Her mother Debra apparently disappeared five years ago. Willy stated his wife had upped and left him. However, at the time Jenny accused her stepfather of murder, presumably because she didn't believe Debra would have left without her. We do know that Willy and Debra weren't getting on at the time of her disappearance. On the face of it, Willy is a prime suspect for the murder of his wife, but they never found a body despite searching extensively. He also denied it at the time and what we heard him say today seems to corroborate that.

'However, we know that Willie had recently decided to tell Jenny something - some kind of news which clearly affected her much worse than he thought it would.' The small man paused, gathering his thoughts.

'Whatever the real story, Kathy Brummel clearly knows something, as does John Dewer.'

'How is it you think John knows more than he's letting on?' asked Emily.

'Remember, Kathy told Willy that she'd spoken to John about cancelling our boat trip and that he'd back up Willy's story.'

'Why would she say that if the ginger nut wasn't in on whatever it is they're in on,' agreed the Admiral.

'We also found that scrap of Velcro on the lantern balcony,' Jimmy reminded them. 'While it doesn't' prove anything other than a red headed person was at some point up in the lantern tower, it does support the theory that John Dewer may well be involved.

'And, Kathy also told Willy that *they'd* be there at nine tomorrow tonight. So, if not John Dewer, then who?'

'So, we think there's a conspiracy of at least three going on, now all we have to do is find out what it is they're hiding,' the Admiral said, standing up. 'Who's for another pint?'

'I'll just goggle again to see if there's anything in the local news about Jenny's death,' Emily decided, pulling her tablet out of her handbag.

'The last time we looked, there was nothing,' Jimmy remembered, getting up to follow the Admiral to the bar, before suddenly turning back. 'Why don't you look up John Dewer while you're at it?' he suggested.

"You could also goggle the local paper for the Dartmoor area?' suggested Mabel. 'The Denmeads live up there don't they? There might be something about them finding the body.'

'Good idea Mabel,' said Emily impressed.

A few minutes later, she looked up excitedly. 'There's a small piece about the accident and a photograph of Iris and Jim Denmead.' She held up her tablet towards Mabel. The picture was of the couple at some kind of festival. The weather looked fine and both of them were dressed in summer attire. 'When was it taken? asked Mabel.

Emily made the picture bigger. 'It says it was in June this year. So, it's quite recent.' She squinted a bit, trying to read the small print without her glasses. 'Apparently they make ice cream which is distributed all over the country.' She looked up thoughtfully. 'I think I might have had one of their ninety nines.'

The Admiral and Jimmy arrived back at the table and the two ladies triumphantly shared their discovery.

'It's a shame we can't get the article printed,' said Jimmy, staring at the picture, 'but in all honesty, I can't think of a possible reason we might give for us wanting it.'

There was a period of silence as the four of them struggled to get their heads around the complex sequence of events.

'Did you find anything out about John Dewer?' Jimmy asked.

'Oh no, I'll have a quick look now.' The other three leant forward as Emily picked up her tablet again. 'You're taking all my light,' she muttered, shooing them back.

'Of course, there's one other possibility,' Jimmy offered while they waited. The others looked over at him.

'We could be imagining the whole conspiracy thing entirely.'

The Admiral snorted. 'So why don't they want us asking any bloody questions?' He shook his head and continued. 'We're not imagining it Jimmy lad, but it's not going to be easy nailing down exactly what happened to Jenny and her mother and being able to prove it.' He paused and took a long draft of his pint before placing it decisively back on the table.

'It says here that John is in partnership with Willy. They run a boat hire business. According to their advert, Morwelly Cruises is the biggest operator of tourist cruises in Morwelly.'

'That's probably because it's the *only* bloody tourist cruise operator in Morwelly,' responded the Admiral, shaking his head.

"It says they have two boats. The Codfather and another one called The Aphrodite.'

'Wasn't that bloody heap of junk we saw Willy on called Aphrodite?' asked the Admiral with a frown.

'I can't remember seeing the name plate,' responded Jimmy, 'but if it was the Aphrodite, the cruising business is clearly not as lucrative as it was.' He nodded down at Emily's tablet. 'And their website is obviously a bit out of date.'

'Well if old Willy's boat shed is anything to go by, he certainly doesn't have a pot to piss in. John Dewer didn't look as if he was wearing hand me downs last night though.' The Admiral paused to think.

'We know something's going to happen at Willy's place tomorrow tonight,' he continued at length. 'The simple fact of the matter is, we've got to be there to see exactly what.'

The others just looked at him wordlessly. The large man frowned at their lack of enthusiasm and opened his mouth to continue, but Jimmy got there first.

'We don't know where he lives Sir,' the small man said, being careful to keep his voice neutral.

'Now that's where you're wrong,' Charles Shackleford responded triumphantly, digging in his pocket for a piece of paper. 'I told Willy we'd still pay him for the trip to help out with the cost of fixing the imaginary problem with his bloody boat. Said I'd get him the cash like we'd arranged and drop it off on our way back to the lighthouse.'

'And he believed you Sir?' Jimmy asked doubtfully, 'Even after everything Kathy said to him this morning?'

'He didn't know we'd been earwigging. We know old Willy at least is short of the readies and to top it all, he spends most of his time in here drinking his troubles away which is bloody costly. 'Course he wanted me to leave it at the boat shed, but I made it clear I wasn't going to leave any money in a bloody shack.

'So he gave me his address...'

∞∞∞

Half an hour and a plate of sandwiches later, the four sleuths were making their way towards the Beach House. They'd concocted the story that they intended to come back to Morwelly in the summer and wanted to inspect the accommodation on offer. There had been no sign of Willy Welbeck or their elderly informant in the Red Lion before they left.

The Beach House was a delightful cottage complete with a thatched roof and winter roses around the porch. A cheerful Christmas wreath hung on the door and a beautifully decorated tree filled the small mullioned window. The Admiral snorted as Emily rang the bell. 'Must have cost her a pretty penny. Wouldn't surprise me if the bloody ghost of Christmas Present comes to let us in,' he muttered as they waited.

'Shut up Scrooge,' snapped Mabel in a rare witty retort, 'I think it looks lovely.' Before the Admiral could respond, the door opened, and Connie Baxter eyed them silently through dark glasses. In complete contrast to her surroundings, the landlady looked as though she was dressed in an old sack - until they realised it was a dressing gown that had clearly seen better days.

For a few seconds they all stared mutely at the apparition in front of them before Emily pulled herself together and said, 'I'm so sorry to bother you Mrs Baxter. Do you remember us? We met last night at the carol concert. I do hope we haven't come at a bad time.' Connie Baxter removed her glasses and all four winced. 'Bloody woman looks like she's been dug up,' the Admiral commented to Jimmy in one of his loud stage whispers, earning him a swift kick in the shin from Mabel.

Connie Baxter was clearly suffering the effects of too much mulled wine and for a few seconds it was touch and go as to whether she even remembered them. Emily was just about to apologise and back away, when sudden recognition appeared in the landlady's bloodshot eyes.

'Yes, yes of course, err, what can I do for you?' Emily glanced over at Mabel who took over. 'We've had a lovely time here in Morwelly,' she gushed in true Mabel fashion, 'so much so that we're thinking of coming again in the summer. We saw your lovely guest house and wondered if we could have a quick look around.' Connie Baxter didn't respond.

'With a view to staying here,' added Emily hurriedly.

'As paying guests,' clarified Jimmy.

'With a discount for booking early,' was the Admiral's contribution, securing him a glare from the other three.

The hungover landlady made a visible effort to pull herself together and stepped back to open the door wider. 'Oh, how nice, please, do come in, I'd love to sit and chat,' she finally managed in a tone that said she'd rather have her toenails pulled out without anaesthetic. Then turning, she hurried down the hall leaving them to presumably follow.

'Are we alright to bring in the dog?' Jimmy called to her departing back.

There was no response and as she'd now disappeared into the depths of the cottage, Mabel, Emily and Jimmy continued to hesitate on the threshold.

'Come on Jimmy lad,' the Admiral's impatience was palpable. 'I'm bloody freezing out here and I need to use the heads. If I hang on any longer my back teeth will be floating.'

'You should have gone in the pub,' admonished Mabel.

'I didn't need to go then. It's being back out in the cold.'

Mabel frowned and shook her head. 'It's not very polite to ask a stranger if you can use their toilet.'

'It's not very bloody polite to pee on their rug either,' responded the Admiral through gritted teeth as he began dancing from foot to foot.

Sighing, Jimmy stepped into the dim hall and led the way towards the back of the cottage where they'd last seen their reluctant hostess. He was disappointed to note that both doors to the two front rooms were firmly closed so offered no opportunity for a quick shufti and they very quickly came to what was clearly a sitting room specifically for guests staying at the Beach House.

Connie Baxter was waiting for them with a strained smile on her face. The room was very quaint, in keeping with the rest of the cottage, but it had the feel and smell of a room that hadn't been used for some time - since the summer Jimmy guessed. Nevertheless, there was another small Christmas tree and few sprigs of holly on the fireplace mantle.

'I'm sorry it's a little chilly in here,' apologised Connie, 'If I'd known you were coming, I'd have laid a fire.'

'Oh, we're perfectly roasting, aren't we Mabel,' responded Emily with a forced smile.

'Warm as toast,' agreed Mabel.

'Positively sweltering,' added Jimmy.

'Have you got a toilet?' asked the Admiral.

The landlady's smile slipped a little, but she nevertheless rallied impressively and told the Admiral to follow her. 'Please make yourselves at home,' she urged the others, 'I'll just pop along and make us some tea.'

'Oh, you don't need to go to any trouble on our account.' Mabel's protest was half hearted at best.

'It's no trouble at all,' Connie responded lightly, finally seeming to get into the swing of things, 'I won't be a moment.'

The Admiral urgently handed Pickles over to Mabel before following the landlady out of the room. As they disappeared back down the hallway, Emily and Mabel seated themselves on the sofa with Pickles curled up happily at their feet while Jimmy began examining the many photographs decorating the walls. They seemed to cover quite an extended time period and he recognised a younger Connie in many of them. While he was browsing, he couldn't help but wonder where Mr. Baxter was or indeed whether there had ever been one. After a few minutes he arrived back at the place he'd started. Most of the photos seemed to be in or around Morwelly. Plainly Connie had lived in the locality for many years.

Frowning, he sat down, the nagging feeling they were missing something still bothering him. Despite their declarations to the contrary, the room really was decidedly chilly, and he rubbed his hands together to generate some warmth. Leaning forward to tuck his hands under his armpits, he noticed the very edge of what looked like a smallish wooden frame peeping out from underneath the sofa in between Mabel and Emily. Quickly getting down onto his hands and knees, he poked at the object, pulling the edge towards him and out from under the sofa.

'What on earth are you doing Jim?' Emily asked peering down at him. Sitting back on his knees Jimmy lifted the photograph he'd unearthed.

It looked to be fairly recent and turning it over, he read, *Will and Debra's wedding day.* Frowning, he turned it back to look at the picture. In the middle were the bride and groom. He could hardly recognise Willy Welbeck. In the photo the man was happy and smiling at his new wife. Debra Welbeck was a pretty petite blonde, the very opposite of her burly husband. Jimmy guessed the event had taken place sometime in the last ten years. In front of the couple stood a serious little girl who he assumed was Jenny. She was wearing a long pale pink frilly dress proclaiming her a bridesmaid, and standing to the side of her were three adult bridesmaids. Jimmy drew in his breath. He recognised the first one as Kathy Brummel, the second was clearly Connie Baxter, and if he wasn't mistaken, the third laughing attendant was Iris Denmead.

Chapter Fifteen

'**W**hy the bloody hell didn't the police pick up on the fact that Iris Denmead knew the Welbecks?' exploded the Admiral when they finally managed to extract themselves from the Beach House.

They were sitting in the car with the heater going full blast passing round Jimmy's phone along with the one set of reading glasses they had between them.

Fortunately, before he'd returned the picture frame back under the sofa, Jimmy had had the foresight to take a quick shot of it with his phone. He'd just had time to sit back down as footsteps sounded in the hall.

When Connie had reappeared with the tray of tea, they'd hardly recognised her. The old dressing gown had been replaced with a smart two piece and her face had been made up within an inch of its life. She poured the tea like a professional, even offering each of them a jammy dodger, and her light-hearted small talk was almost an art form. The only moment her aplomb slipped slightly was at the Admiral's comment on her change of appearance on returning from the bathroom. 'Bloody hell, what happened to the bride of Dracula?'

She recovered her composure admirably however and actually managed to respond by wagging her finger at him and giving a tinkling laugh. Even the Admiral had been impressed when she managed to get them to leave a deposit for a booking they had no intention of taking...

'The police may well have been aware of the connection Sir

for all we know,' Jimmy responded taking back his phone. 'The problem is, how do we find out? If we go waltzing into the local police station asking questions, the plod are going to want to know how we know and why we're asking. We daren't show our hand too soon Sir. As it is, we have no proof of any wrongdoing.'

'Apart from a bloody great porky told to the police,' muttered the Admiral.

'We think,' added Jimmy.

Charles Shackleford took a deep breath. 'I hate to say it Jimmy lad, but our only option really is to be at Willy's tomorrow night at nine sharp and find out once and for all what the bloody hell is going on.'

This time there was no argument from Jimmy, Emily or Mabel. There was a sense that whatever they'd got themselves into was coming to a head and all three were equally keen to try to get to the bottom of the mystery and get back to celebrating Christmas.

'We'll drop the fifty pounds off at Willy's place now,' the Admiral decided. 'That way we can do a quick recce while it's still light.'

'Have you got the post code Sir?' asked Jimmy.

'No, I haven't got the bloody post code,' the Admiral retorted. 'It was looking for the bollocking post code that got us into this mess in the first place.'

'I thought you were enjoying this whole business,' countered Emily, 'and it was definitely you Charlie Shackleford who proposed *Operation Lighthouse*,' she reminded him.

'I know, I know,' sighed the Admiral, 'it's just difficult to stay enthusiastic about something when it involves freezing your pecker off.'

'You're not wrong there, Sir,' agreed Jimmy leaning forward to turn the heating up, before looking down at his phone again. 'So, what's the address again?'

Five minutes later they were heading towards Willy's house which was situated a few hundred yards past the edge of the village. Predictably their suspect's home turned out to be an old farmhouse that had seen better days. It was surrounded on three sides by a ramshackle hedge and on the fourth a large decrepit barn.

'Right then,' the Admiral said turning off the engine. 'You ladies stay here in the warmth while me and Jimmy have a quick shufti.'

'That's very sweet of you dear,' responded Mabel. 'Are you going to take Pickles with you?'

Jimmy frowned. 'What do you think Sir? We'll only be a few minutes. We don't want to be spotted snooping around.'

The Admiral looked down at the springer sitting between the two women. His ears were perked up and his tail wagging non-stop. 'We'll take him with us,' the large man decided. 'Just in case we get in to trouble. Come on boy.'

The two men climbed out of the car, quickly shutting the doors to prevent the warmth from escaping. Keeping Pickles on the lead, the Admiral led the way towards the gate and the pathway leading to the house beyond.

'The barn looks to be empty,' observed Jimmy as they walked past the dark cavernous entrance. 'Might provide us with a good hideout later while we wait for the action to start.'

'Good idea,' agreed the Admiral, clearly regaining his enthusiasm for *Operation Lighthouse*. 'We'll aim to be here about eightish so we can make sure we're in position.'

They arrived at the front door and hesitated for a few seconds, wondering whether to knock. There were no cars around and no lights on in the house - nothing to indicate there was someone inside. Charles Shackleford looked down at Pickles to see if the spaniel was picking up anything interesting other than the smell of rabbits. While the hound's nose was eagerly glued to the ground, he gave no indication there were any alien noises within earshot.

'You go that way round and I'll go this way,' the Admiral ordered Jimmy. 'We'll have a quick shufti through the windows, get a feel for the layout of the place before we post the cash through the letterbox and bugger off.' Jimmy nodded without replying and they crept off in opposite directions.

Meanwhile Mabel and Emily huddled together as the inside of the car grew slowly colder. 'What on earth are they doing,' muttered Emily when ten minutes had gone by.

'I hope nothing bad has happened,' fretted Mabel peering out into the developing gloom.

Nothing happened for another couple of minutes, then to Emily and Mabel's relief, the two men appeared together round the side of the house.

Of Pickles there was no sign.

'We can't just leave him,' cried Mabel as the Admiral started the car.

'Of course, we're not going to bloody leave him,' responded the Admiral.

'How on earth did you lose him in the first place?' Emily asked anxiously

'He was sniffing round the lawn at the back of the house and kept whining, so I let him off the lead to have a proper nose. The bloody grass was so overgrown, I lost sight of him. When I managed to spot him again, he was picking something up in his mouth, then he looked back at me and suddenly took off back in the direction of the village. It was only a few minutes ago, so we should be able to catch up with him.'

'Surely we'd be better to wait here for him to come back,' argued Mabel, nearly in tears.

'We can't hang around here now Mabel,' the Admiral said driving back towards the main road. 'If we're spotted, the whole bollocking game is up and we'll never find out the truth of what happened to Jenny Welbeck or her mother.'

'Maybe it's time to take it to the police,' said Emily.

'We have nothing to take them except a load of speculation,' argued Jimmy. 'We have to see this through.'

'Well I'm telling you now Charles Shackleford,' Mabel stated leaning forward to poke the Admiral in the back for emphasis, 'if anything happens to Pickles, I will never ever forgive you. And there'll be no wedding either.'

'Nothing will happen to him,' stated the Admiral firmly, although he was unable to hide his anxiety entirely. 'Now stop gassing and keep your eyes peeled.'

As Charles Shackleford drove slowly back towards Morwelly, the other three peered out of the windows into the gathering gloom.

They were almost back at the edge of the village when suddenly Jimmy spotted a dark shape running in the direction of the harbour. 'THERE HE IS,' shouted the small man excitedly.

'Why the bloody hell is he going that way?' frowned the Admiral as Pickles turned into the narrow cobbled street leading down to the quay. After hurriedly stopping the car, he and Jimmy climbed out and started after the disappearing dog. 'PICKLES, HERE BOY,' yelled the Admiral breaking into a trot.

Five minutes later, they arrived at the wharf, just in time to see Pickles vanish into the derelict boat they'd seen Willy on earlier. Luckily the quayside was deserted.

'What a bloody cake and arse party,' rasped the Admiral stopping and bending forward to get his breath back.

'There doesn't look to be anybody on the boat,' observed Jimmy as he peered in through the porthole window.

'Can you see Pickles?' wheezed the Admiral.

Jimmy was about to say no, when suddenly the spaniel appeared on the deck, his tail wagging ecstatically at seeing them both. Jumping back onto the quayside, Pickles danced excitedly between the two men before dropping something at his master's feet.

'What have you got there boy?' the Admiral murmured, cursing the fact that he hadn't got his glasses. Bending down he picked up what looked like a small stick and held it up in the air for Jimmy to see. 'What do you think this is?' he asked his friend with a frown.

Jimmy trotted over, fumbling around in his coat pocket for his glasses. Once on his nose, he took the object from the Admiral and held it up, narrowing his eyes to see it better in the fading light.

'Oh, no Sir.' His horrified whisper sent a shiver down the Admiral's spine.

'What the hell is it Jimmy lad?' There was a small silence, then, 'I think it's a human finger.'

The two men stared at each other in shocked silence. 'So why did Pickles bring the bloody thing back here?' the Admiral questioned when he'd managed to find his voice again. Jimmy was busy wrapping the grisly object in a handkerchief he'd dug out of this pocket.

The Admiral frowned. 'I hope that's a clean hanky Jimmy, that finger's crucial evidence. It's got DNA on it.'

'It's been in a dog's mouth after rotting in Willy's garden for God knows how long,' retorted Jimmy. 'They'll be lucky if they manage to prove it's bloody human.'

Jimmy's voice cracked, indicating his level of anxiety and the Admiral was about to offer his insubordinate a little support when Pickles began whining. 'What's wrong boy?' he said instead to the agitated dog. Pickles backed away, tail still wagging then turned and jumped back onto the derelict Aphrodite.

'I think he wants to show us something Sir,' murmured Jimmy.

The Admiral looked around the deserted harbour. The light was really failing now and the cold was becoming biting. 'Let's have a quick shufti then,' he said to Jimmy. 'We're the only numpties daft enough to be out here in this weather anyway.'

The two men clambered aboard. Once on deck, Pickles wasted no time in disappearing down into the dark of the cabin. Glancing at the Admiral, Jimmy took the lead and made his way towards the cockpit. Once there he peered down into the stygian blackness, waiting for his eyes to adjust to the gloom. The hatch had obviously been broken at some point and hung drunkenly against the ladder and the only sound was that of Pickles' soft whining down in the companionway.

'Right Sir, if you don't object, then I'll go first,' Jimmy whispered. The Admiral waved him on and hesitantly the small man turned and made his way backwards down the rickety ladder. A few minutes later they were both standing hesitantly at the entrance to the decrepit saloon. 'I've got a torch on my phone,' murmured Jimmy digging around in his jacket for his mobile. The torchlight revealed a cabin that didn't look as if it had been used in decades. The upholstery of the fitted seats was covered in mould and thick green algae covered the porthole windows casting an almost demonic light over the room. Pickles was scratching urgently on a door at the other end. With Jimmy holding the torch, the Admiral made his way towards the dog, carefully avoiding the debris on the floor. Without waiting, he took hold of the handle and pushed hard.

Expecting resistance, the large man nearly fell headlong into the revealed space as the door into what was clearly the aft cabin opened easily. The reason for the well-oiled hinges was quickly apparent however. Someone wanted to be able to come in and out of the small cabin quickly and noiselessly.

Whoever it was had obviously been using the abandoned boat for storage because inside the room, barely visible on the filthy floor lay a desiccated foot.

Chapter Sixteen

The Admiral stared down at their second gruesome find - all thanks to Pickles.

His voice was hoarse as he called out to Jimmy. While not squeamish under normal circumstances, it was hard not to queasy at the sight in front of him. As Jimmy joined him in the doorway, the Admiral pointed to the floor. 'Some poor bugger's definitely missing a few body parts,' was all he said as the small man shone his torch on the ground and bent down to take a closer look.

'We've got to assume that both of these err... limbs have come from the same person,' Jimmy murmured after couple of minutes. 'Neither look to be particularly fresh - in fact they look almost mummified, and there's not much of a smell either.'

'Well Pickles definitely caught a wiff,' interrupted the Admiral.

'Dogs have a much keener smell than we do,' reasoned Jimmy, 'and I'm definitely not an expert as you well know Sir.' The small man paused before continuing, 'But still, I'd hazard a guess that the foot has been parted from whatever leg it came from for quite some time.' He looked up at the Admiral, all but invisible in the dark. 'Both the finger and the foot look to have been removed with a sharp object so I think it's safe to assume that whoever they belonged to is dead.'

'Well, we can't just leave someone's severed bloody foot lying around, so we need something to put it in,' Charles Shackleford commented, 'then we can scarper - the sooner the better. This place is seriously giving me the heebie jeebies. It's like a bloody horror film.' His voice was filled with a dread that was beginning to consume them both. The dark felt like a living breathing entity and the open hatch at their back a perfect invitation to a nameless knife wielding maniac.

Nodding his head, Jimmy quickly shone his torch around for something to wrap their grisly trophy in. At length he spied an old pillowcase lying forgotten on the bunk and taking a deep breath, he plunged his hand inside and gingerly picked up the foot, turning the pillowcase inside out, leaving the limb inside.

Without further ado, they made their way carefully through the main cabin and back up the ladder to the cockpit, this time with the Admiral leading the way. Charles Shackleford stuck his head out of the hatch cautiously to check they were still alone, before climbing out the rest of the way and Jimmy quickly followed suit. Pickles once again gave lie to his advancing years by simply jumping up through the opening and beating them onto the quayside where he stood wagging his tail as the Admiral put him back on the lead muttering that he hoped the spaniel hadn't seen fit to eat any bits.

A couple of minutes later, they were making their way back up the cobbled street to the parked car.

∞∞∞

'I think we should take them to the police,' Emily stated faintly, refusing to look at the two mummified body parts lying on the coffee table in their cosy sitting room back at the lighthouse.

'Technically we shouldn't even have touched the damn foot, just stayed on the boat and called the police from there,' responded Jimmy, 'but I think I'm right in saying Sir that neither of us wanted to hang around long enough for the plod to get there.'

The Admiral nodded his emphatic agreement. 'I for one had no wish to bump into some nutter capable of hacking off someone's bollocking foot and God knows what other bits of him.'

'Or her,' offered Mabel helpfully.

Jimmy leant forward to examine the foot again. 'If it belongs to a woman,' he mused, 'she's got pretty big feet.'

'Right then, what have we got to connect Willie and the rest of his cronies to these body parts?' asked the Admiral.

'You found the finger in his garden and the foot on his boat,' stated Emily acidly, 'Surely that's enough to make sure they're all questioned by the police.'

'Oh, they'll want to have a word with Willy at least,' agreed the Admiral, 'but there's nothing to connect the others and I've got a feeling these bits we've got here are the tip of the bloody iceberg.'

'The connection's all circumstantial at best, certainly at the moment,' added Jimmy.

'I know it's the last bloody thing we want to do Jimmy, but I say again, we've got to go back over to Willy's place and finish *Operation Lighthouse* tomorrow night,' continued the Admiral thumping the coffee table for emphasis and causing the finger to bounce as though still alive.

Mabel instinctively took a step back. 'Don't you think *Operation Lighthouse* might have gone a bit too far,' she murmured anxiously.

'I think the Admiral's right Mabel,' Jimmy responded, 'we have to finish what we've started. He turned back to his former commanding officer. 'But I really do think it should just be me and you heading out tomorrow night Sir,' he added, glancing over at Emily and Mabel. The Admiral was about to nod his agreement when both ladies came out with an explosive, 'No.'

'If you think we're sitting here waiting and worrying whether you're going to end up losing a part of your anatomy, then you've got another think coming Jim Noon,' stated Emily, her voice leaving no room for argument.

'We're coming with you,' agreed Mabel, 'and what's more, so is Pickles. He saved your bacon last year during *Operation Murderous Marriages* and he led us to this... this evidence too.' She waved a distasteful hand at the desiccated parts still sitting on the coffee table.

The two ladies stared belligerently at their other halves, daring them to argue.

The Admiral glanced over at Jimmy, then sighed in unaccustomed submission. 'Right then, if you're coming, we need to work on a plan tonight. Then tomorrow we'll head into Ilfracombe to get some camouflage gear.'

Jimmy gave a silent prayer of thanks that on this occasion the Admiral hadn't thought to bring his combat gear. The last time his former commanding officer had worn it was during a half-baked scouting mission at his son-in-law's house. Of course, at the time, Noah Westbrook had simply been Hollywood's golden boy and not yet a relation. Nevertheless, Charles Shackleford's geriatric mutant ninja turtle ensemble was still the talk of their local pub - mostly, it had to be said, when the Admiral wasn't around...

While Mabel and Emily went to work rustling up some sausage and mash, the Admiral used the grubby pillowcase, to gingerly pick up the foot and the finger and, wrapping the sheet up tightly, went to place them in the fridge.

'Don't leave those horrible things anywhere near the bacon,' ordered Emily with a shudder.

By seven thirty they were seated at the table tucking into the perfect fodder in the Admiral's opinion to get the old grey matter working overtime. Once the table was cleared away, the ladies pulled out a box of *Quality Street* as they got to work.

'I want us to be in place no later than twenty hundred hours tomorrow night,' the Admiral stated. 'That means we need to muster here no later than nineteen thirty. We'll then have thirty minutes to get into position so we've got another hour to get ourselves sorted before Kathy whatshername and the others turn up. We'll park the car as close as we can to Willy's place but we might end up with a bit of a hike so it's important we all have the right footwear.'

'Emily, remember your bunion,' commented Mabel turning to her friend in concern before helping herself to another sweet.

'We really don't know what to expect,' Jimmy added gravely to Mabel and Emily, although he had to speak up a bit to be heard over the sucking as Mabel went to work on a toffee penny. 'So, it's important you ladies follow every order without question.' Emily nodded dutifully and patted her concerned husband on his arm before asking Mabel if she'd kindly pass her a coffee cream. Then she turned back to the Admiral and asked if he'd finished yet because the *Dr Who Christmas Special* was just about to start...

The next morning saw them all up bright and early. The Admiral and Jimmy because they were eager to solve the mystery and call time on *Operation Lighthouse,* and Mabel and Emily because they had an opportunity to go shopping.

Leaving Pickles in the warmth of the lighthouse, they drove over to the large seaside resort of Ilfracombe. Once they'd parked the car in the town centre, the two ladies excitedly insisted they be allowed to go off on their own to choose their camouflage gear. After his protests fell on deaf ears, Jimmy gave Mabel and Emily strict instructions that under no circumstances were they to buy anything that wasn't black. Then, watching them totter off, he felt the familiar tug of anxiety.

The feeling intensified when the Admiral turned to him enthusiastically and said, 'Right then Jimmy what do you think to a swift pint before we head over to the nearest charity shop?'

In the event, Jimmy needn't have worried. The trip to Ilfracombe proved so successful that they were back in the lighthouse with a fish and chip supper before it began to get dark and even more impressive, they were all ready to go well before the nineteen thirty deadline.

All four were dressed head to toe in black. The Admiral muttered that it was a good job they were aiming to be invisible as Mabel appeared to be sporting a large black onesie with a hood so big he could hardly see her face inside it.

'Don't worry about me being cold Charlie,' she said, mistaking the Admiral's look for one of concern, 'I've got two pairs of tights and my thermal long johns underneath this, along with a vest and that sweater of yours I accidentally shrunk in the wash.' She partially unzipped the onesie in case he needed proof. 'I've been looking for that bloody jumper,' the Admiral remarked with a frown.

Emily on the other hand was dressed very stylishly in a fitted black jumpsuit reminiscent of the late *Diana Rigg* in her *Avengers* heyday. In fact, Jimmy felt a little stirring the like of which he hadn't felt for a good few years and he made a mental note to ask Emily if she'd wear the outfit again the next time they had occasion to go on a night out to Bingo. Unfortunately, the shoes were not entirely *Emma Peel* being in fact a pair of extra-large wellies to accommodate her bunion, but Jimmy was more than happy to keep his eyes further up.

Both the Admiral and Jimmy had succeeded in purchasing their camouflage outfits from the second charity shop they ventured into. The only downside was the bright orange logo that decorated the back of each declaring their former use as uniforms for a local plumbing company. A black marker pen did a good job of masking most of the lettering, and they now merely resembled rejects from the *Men in Black*. Underneath the jackets they'd donned black thermal fisherman's sweaters, and finally, black balaclavas finished their ensemble.

Both men were now sweating profusely.

'Right then, Jimmy, torch, weapon?'

'Check,' the small man answered, holding up his torch and trusty rounders bat.

'Mabel?' The matron proudly brandished an ancient bottle of *Charlie* perfume which unfortunately had no spray. 'What do you intend to do - sprinkle them with it?' the Admiral commented. Sighing, he reached into his ditty bag and brought out the old can of pepper spray he and Jimmy had used to such effect in *Operation Murderous Marriages* a year earlier.

'Emily?' Charles Shackleford barked, only to back up slightly as Emily brandished a knife large enough to cut someone's head off.

Jimmy paled before saying carefully, 'Sweetheart, I'm not sure where you'll be able to store such a large weapon without doing yourself an injury.'

'I thought I'd stick it inside my boot,' responded Emily, her bottom lip jutting out mulishly.

'Oh Emily,' said Mabel with a slight shudder, 'I know you want to get rid of your bunion dear, but I wouldn't have thought accidently slicing it off in the middle of a clandestine operation was the way to go about it.' Emily frowned mutinously.

'I mean, it would ruin your lovely outfit. You can't get blood out of anything,' Mabel continued seriously.

'Here my love,' Jimmy offered quickly, 'Why don't you use this one. It has a cover and you can pop it in your welly without any danger to yourself.' The knife he handed over was as blunt as a spoon. Jimmy knew that because he'd used it to peel the potatoes the day before. It could still do a bit of damage if necessary though he reasoned.

'Right then if you lot have finished arsing around, let's get *Operation Lighthouse* over and done with,' Charles Shackleford said decisively, bending down to clip on Pickles' lead.

∞∞∞

After parking the car in the shadowy entrance to a deserted field, they all climbed silently out. Even Pickles only made the occasional soft huff as put his nose to the ground. They were about fifty yards away from their destination and the car was shielded from any prying eyes by the overgrown hedgerow. Jimmy handed Emily his torch, instructing her to use it only when absolutely necessary. Emily nodded and promptly shone it straight into her husband's eyes. 'Make sure to keep the beam pointing towards the ground,' he advised with a wince.

The Admiral fished his torch out of the boot along with his old walking stick - a very effective weapon as Jimmy had previously discovered to his cost - then turned back to his crime solving companions and ordered them to synchronise watches.

'I make it nineteen forty six hours,' he informed them in a stage whisper that could have been heard in the Red Lion. Jimmy sighed, the feeling of impending doom settling over him like a shroud.

'I'll go first with Pickles,' continued the Admiral. 'Jimmy, you take up the rear.' The small man nodded, and they turned in single file to make their way as quietly as possible to Willy Welbeck's house.

Just before they reached the gate, Mabel suddenly stopped with a stifled scream. 'I think I've trodden in something,' she moaned. The Admiral shone his torch down at her feet. 'Bloody hell Mabel,' he muttered as the light illuminated her foot enveloped right up to her ankle in a large cow pat.

'Lift your foot up carefully,' advised Emily with a slight shudder, 'otherwise you might lose your trainer.'

'Bugger, bugger, bugger,' Mabel muttered crossly as she slowly pulled her foot out of the soggy mire. 'These trainers were my Christmas present from Charlie.'

'Were they?' questioned her beloved in surprise.

'Come on, let's keep going,' hissed Jimmy impatiently.

Unfortunately, Mabel was now walking as though she had one leg six inches shorter than the other giving a very good impersonation of *Boris Karloff* in his prime. It didn't help that Pickles clearly regarded the disgusting mess on Mabel's shoe as a bit of a snack.

They finally arrived at the dilapidated barn without any further mishaps. Sneaking inside, the foursome gathered together for a whispered recce.

'The lights are on, so it looks as though someone's in the house,' observed Jimmy. 'What do you think Sir? Do we wait here to see who turns up or do we have a quick shufti now to see if we can find out who's in there already?'

The Admiral frowned and scratched his head under the balaclava. 'If we were back in Borneo, I'd be inclined to think I had a couple of Bombay runners up there,' he muttered to himself, mulling over Jimmy's words.

'We really need to get an idea of how many we're dealing with,' he answered eventually, 'and see if we can get a look at 'em.

'We'd better go now though,' he continued, shining his torch down on his watch. 'By my reckoning, the whole cake and arse party is due to kick off in about forty-five minutes. Jimmy lad, you come with me. Mabel, you and Emily stay here with Pickles.'

The two men cautiously made their way towards the house. Apart from the lights illuminating the small area around the building, the darkness was almost absolute. There was very little light pollution and for the most part they were walking almost blind. Neither spoke, too busy concentrating on keeping to the path. Venturing into Willy's overgrown garden could potentially result in a broken ankle or worse. As they approached the front door, they saw a shadow walk through the hall to the room on the right. The person who became visible in the living room window was unsurprisingly Willy Welbeck. They froze, watching and waiting. In the ensuing silence, they could hear arguing. Willy was obviously talking to somebody and he was most definitely not happy.

The Admiral glanced over at Jimmy, who'd become more distinct in the shadows nearer the house. He was just about to speak, when the small man put his finger up to his lips and pointed back towards the window.

Another person had entered the room. They could tell it was a woman and from the faint voices and her angry gestures, she was clearly the one Willy was arguing with. The two men waited in the shadows, hardly daring to breathe, but no one else came into the room. After a few seconds, the woman threw up her hands and turned to retrace her steps.

For a few seconds they were able to see her face clearly. It was Debra Welbeck.

Mabel and Emily waited anxiously in the barn as the Admiral and Jimmy were swallowed by the dark.

'I'm beginning to think we're a bit too old for any operation that doesn't include a couple of weeks relaxation in a hospital bed,' murmured Mabel, tucking her hood around her face for warmth.

'Nonsense Mabel,' Emily retorted, 'We've never had so much fun and you know it.' Despite her spirited response, Mabel sensed a note of misgiving in Emily's words and glanced over at her friend. Unfortunately, she couldn't see anything other than a vague outline and contented herself by fumbling for Emily's hand and gripping it tightly. At that moment, Pickles began to whine.

'What is it boy?' Mabel asked bending down to stroke the spaniel's soft ears. Her heart thudded apprehensively as Pickles began pulling on his lead. Not out into the night after his master, but deeper into the blackness of the barn.

'It's alright Pickles, there's nothing to be scared of,' whispered Mabel doing her best to comfort the dog whose hackles were beginning to rise. To her relief, the spaniel stopped pulling and nuzzled into her hand. For a moment the silence was complete. The two ladies listened carefully, but the only sound they could hear was their breathing and Pickles' soft panting.

Just as they began to relax, Pickles started whining and pulling again.

'Do you think he can sense something?' whispered Emily uneasily.

'I don't know,' Mabel whispered back. 'Should I let him go?'

Emily shook her head, adding, 'No,' when she realised Mabel couldn't see her. 'If we let him off the lead, he could do another runner and then we'll be completely scuppered.' She paused as the springer began to pull more insistently. 'I think we've got to let him lead us to whatever's bothering him.'

Both ladies stared into the dark. 'We could fall over and break our necks,' Mabel muttered anxiously. 'I know I mentioned a relaxing stint in hospital, but I'm not wearing my best underwear.'

In answer, Emily fished in her tracksuit pocket and triumphantly brought out Jimmy's torch. Carefully pointing it to the floor, she turned it on, then, glancing over at Mabel's now ghostly face, she directed the beam towards the back of the barn. In response, Pickles upped his game and began dancing about, alternately whining and growling.

'Can you see anything?' murmured Mabel, allowing Pickles to

pull her forward. Emily shook her head and allowed the beam to play across the back wall. Initially they thought the barn was completely empty, apart from some mouldy hay covering the floor, but as the spaniel led them insistently towards the far-left hand corner, they noticed the straw there was piled higher.

Mabel allowed Pickles to pull her towards the mound of rotten hay while Emily followed, holding the light steady. As they approached, Pickles whining became frantic and once he was close enough, he jumped headlong into the heap, sending bits mouldy straw flying everywhere. 'Ugh,' cried Emily jumping back, completely forgetting to whisper in her disgust.

Triumphantly, Pickles began scrabbling against something that sounded hollow. 'What is it boy? What have you found?' Mabel murmured, plucking up the courage to approach. Pulling hard on the spaniel's lead, she finally managed to separate him from whatever it was he'd unearthed.

Emily moved closer, shining the torchlight on an old, damp cardboard box that was slowly collapsing inwards. Taking a deep breath as she reached the object, she shone the light down. Pickles had successfully demolished the lid, fully exposing the contents within. Emily gave a small scream which she hastily covered with her hand.

The box undoubtedly contained the rest of the poor unfortunate whose foot and finger they currently had stored in their fridge.

Chapter Seventeen

Emily and Mabel stared in horrified fascination at the mummified remains.

There didn't appear to be much of a smell, just a slightly sweet and musty aroma that was bearable.

All of a sudden, they heard a noise behind them. Turning in sudden fear at being discovered, Emily instinctively swung the torch beam towards the entrance, while Pickles let out a small yip.

'Turn that bollocking light off Emily, do you want the whole bloody world to know we're holed up in somebody's barn?'

'Oh, thank the Lord you're here,' Mabel breathed, nearly in tears.

'Are you alright?' asked Emily, once more dipping the torch to the floor at their feet.

Jimmy nodded. 'Whoever the foot and finger belong to,' he stated, 'it's definitely not Debra Welbeck...'

...'Because as of five minutes ago she was alive and kicking in Willy's living room,' interrupted the Admiral, clearly unable to stop himself from delivering the punchline.

To both men's surprise, Mabel and Emily seemed less than impressed by their discovery of Debra Welbeck's miraculous reincarnation and instead of asking questions, Emily swung the torch back to an old carboard box at their feet. 'You need to see this,' was all she said, her voice sounding strangely husky.

The two men quickly made their way to the back of the barn, only to stare wordlessly at the revealed contents of the box. Eventually, it was the Admiral who spoke first.

'Right then, it's no good us acting like lost farts in a haunted milk bottle, the stakes have just got a bloody sight higher. I think it's finally time to get the plod involved. What do you say Jimmy?'

'I think we're safe to say that the 'thing' Willy wanted finished tonight was the disposing of this body. We think we've got his foot and one finger, but I don't think the rest of the cadaver is here. It's my guess that after chopping whoever it is up, they've been moving bits and pieces gradually and burying them separately.'

'Well it's taken them a long bloody time,' the Admiral muttered. 'Surely it doesn't take five bollocking years to dispose of a corpse.'

'At this stage, we don't actually know when this person died,' argued Jimmy, 'although I'd agree by the state of decomposition, it wasn't recently.'

'Well I can see how that finger Pickles found ended up in the garden,' Emily said with a shudder, 'but how on earth did the foot end up on the boat?'

'Maybe all the bits were on the boat originally,' mused Jimmy. 'It could be our victim was killed there.'

'If he or she was, there's got to be some kind of evidence on board,' added the Admiral.

'In addition to the foot, which we unfortunately removed,' offered Jimmy drily.

'Can we carry the box back to the car?' asked Mabel.

Jimmy shook his head. 'We can't move any more of the evidence or we could be accused of tampering. I think you're right Sir, we need to bring in the police.' He rummaged in his pocket searching for his phone. 'Bugger, I think I've left it in the car.'

'What do you mean you've left your bloody phone in the car? You need to get a damn grip man, you'll be on dishwasher duty when all this is finished if you don't buck up.'

'I'm sorry Sir,' answered Jimmy with a sigh. 'You've got to admit things have been a little tense over the last few hours.'

The Admiral hmphed. 'Well, you'll just have to go and fetch it,' the large man stated in a tone that brooked no argument.

Jimmy frowned. 'Can't we just use yours Sir,' he asked.

The Admiral gave his former Master at Arms *the Look*. 'I haven't got it.'

'Well where is it?' asked Mabel.

'It doesn't damn well matter where it is,' the Admiral answered before drawing himself up pompously. 'As the senior responsible officer for this operation, it's my job to give the orders. I'm not a bloody receptionist.'

'No, you're a bloody idiot,' snapped Emily.

'Any more comments like that and I'll send you over the Wall,' warned the Admiral, outraged at the affront of the woman.

'You haven't got the authority to send me anywhere Charlie Shackleford, you're not in the Navy anymore,' Emily hissed.

'So, can we use your phone Emily?' Mabel hurriedly interrupted, before they got as far as pistols at dawn.

There was a pause. 'I haven't got it,' responded Emily primly.

'Ha,' exploded the Admiral, all need for silence completely forgotten.

Sighing with frustration, Jimmy stepped between them. 'Enough,' he barked using his best Master at Arms voice. Once they'd subsided to a sulky silence, he turned to Mabel. 'Have you got your phone with you,' he asked hopefully.

The matron shook her head. 'I left it on charge,' she whispered apologetically.

All four stared at each other, having finally run out of words.

'What a load of Horlicks,' the Admiral muttered eventually in defeat.

Jimmy took a deep breath. 'It's not such a big problem,' he said, 'I'll simply go back to the car and call the police from there.' He turned to the Admiral. 'I'll only be gone half an hour or so Sir. If I leg it now, I'll get out before the others turn up. Once all the suspects are present, it will be over to the plod to deal with them. We've gone as far as we can.'

The Admiral nodded his approval. 'There you go Jimmy lad, self-adjusting cock up. We'll keep an eye on these bits and pieces, but I'd have thought the culprits are unlikely to make a beeline straight over here. They'll muster in the house first. We'll make sure to keep our heads low until the plod turn up.' He turned back to look down at the sad remains in the box. 'I wonder who the poor bugger is?' he questioned shaking his head, 'and more importantly which one of the blighters did the deed and why?'

Unexpectedly, they heard the sound of distant voices. 'Quick, turn the light off,' hissed the Admiral.

After the small circle of light, the darkness was almost smothering. They waited at the back of the barn in tense silence as the voices gradually got louder.

'They're early,' muttered the Admiral glancing futilely down at his invisible watch. 'Damn and bollocks, I didn't hear a bloody car.'

'Fumbling behind him, Jimmy managed to take hold of Emily's hand. Leaning towards her, he whispered, 'You and Mabel back yourselves right up into the other corner and sit down,' he ordered urgently. 'Put your heads down between your knees and, providing we're far enough away, your black clothes should hide you.'

'But what about you?' protested Emily.

'If they come into the barn, they'll collar us anyway.' Jimmy gave his wife a small push. He heard her soft sniffle as she took hold of her friend's arm. The Admiral patted Mabel's hand as she handed Pickles' lead to him.

'Come on Sir, let's move away from this corner. If they do come in, we'll need to stall them as long as possible.'

'I think you should make a run for it Jimmy lad,' the Admiral murmured as they stepped carefully towards the entrance, watching the bobbing torchlights come gradually closer. 'You're a bit of a short arse, so if you slip out now, they might not spot you.'

'I don't want to leave the three of you at the mercy of a bunch of murdering rustics,' Jimmy responded, his reluctance clear.

'It's too bloody late for that Jimmy lad. The only way we're going to avoid juggling halos is to get the police down here as soon as possible.'

'We might be wrong about everything,' muttered Jimmy desperately.

'If we are, then I'll happily admit we dropped a bollock for wasting police time.' The Admiral fished in his pocket. 'Here are the keys Jimmy. Now get your arse in gear while you still can.

That's an order.'

Jimmy took a deep breath and saluted in the gloom. Then creeping to the entrance, he slipped noiselessly to the side and let the darkness swallow him up.

The small man had managed to escape just in time. Only a few seconds later, the Admiral was blinded by a torch shining directly in his face.

'What the bloody hell are you doing here?' The Admiral shielded his eyes, trying to see who'd spoken. Luckily, the torch was lowered and after blinking for a few seconds he was able to make out four people. Predicably one of them was Willy Welbeck. He recognised the others as Kathy Brummel, Connie Baxter and John Dewer. There was no sign of Debra Welbeck.

'So, where's the wife then Willy?' Charles Shackleford stated bluntly. 'I've never seen such a bloody healthy-looking dead woman.'

'I never claimed she was dead,' was Willy's nervous response.

'You told the police you didn't know where she was though, and I doubt you managed to lose her in your bloody living room.' Part of him knew he was skating on thin ice by goading the man, but the Admiral reasoned the longer he could keep them all talking, the more time he was giving Jimmy.

'Enough,' barked Kathy Brummel. 'What exactly are you doing here Mr. Shackleford? This is private property.' Her voice was icy and the Admiral had no problem imagining her offing someone she didn't like.

John Dewer took a step forward. "Mr Shackleford, I can't imagine what your purpose is in hiding out in a dilapidated barn, but perhaps now would be a good time for you to leave. As Kathy told you, this is private property.' His tone was cool but pleasant in complete contrast to his companion.

The Admiral took a deep breath. If he left now, not only would he be abandoning Mabel and Emily - who by hiding in the corner of the barn were all but admitting they'd seen something they shouldn't - he'd be leaving the murdering bunch to dispose of whoever was in the bloody cardboard box, and they'd never be brought to justice. He glanced down at his watch. By his estimation, Jimmy had been gone for a little over five minutes.

'What are you waiting for?'

Charles Shackleford made a split decision to come clean, see if he could shake anyone into some kind of a confession. At the very least, it would keep them talking. He couldn't see any obvious firearms in the torchlight.

'Think it's a bit bloody late to send me off with a flea in my ear.' he said, 'Especially if you're worried I might stumble across the grisly secret you've got stashed away in the corner.'

Willy took a step forward to stand next to John, his hands held out in front of him in a conciliatory gesture. 'It's not what you think,' he countered desperately.

'It doesn't matter what he thinks.' A new voice joined in the discussion as Debra Welbeck walked into the barn. She was carrying an old shotgun which was pointed right at him. 'He's not going to get an opportunity to tell anyone.'

The Admiral felt himself come out in a cold sweat. For the first time he wondered if he might be truly done for. Then he squared his shoulders. He was an Admiral in the Royal Navy for Nelson's sake and he'd be damned if his final moments were going to be in a crumbling barn. He hadn't even managed to get Mabel down the bloody aisle yet.

'Cracking plan,' he commented scathingly. 'And do you think you'll have another five years to bury bits of me all over the bloody countryside?'

'I have no idea what you're talking about,' said Debra coldly. 'You were trespassing on private property and I mistook you for an intruder.

'*Officer he was carrying a gun,*' she parodied with a smirk. 'I can be very persuasive when I have to be.'

'You're bloody right about that,' answered the Admiral. 'Did you *persuade* your daughter to throw herself off Whitebeam lighthouse or perhaps even give her a helping hand?'

For a second he thought he'd gone too far. Debra Welbeck stepped forward and lifted her gun. 'You have no fucking idea what you're talking about, you doddering old fart,' she spat.

The Admiral frowned. He didn't mind being called a fart - throughout his career he'd been called far worse - but doddering? *That* he objected to.

He felt the lead in his hand begin to vibrate. Up to now Pickles had been quiet with the exception of the occasional grumble but now he began to growl in earnest.

'So, enlighten me,' he continued, holding tightly onto the spaniel's lead, 'If you're going to kill me anyway, at least tell me who killed that poor bugger behind me and why?'

Connie Baxter spoke up for the first time, her voice so low, the Admiral could hardly hear her. 'It was an accident,' she whispered.

'Shut up Connie,' said Kathy sharply.

'Why the hell are we still covering this up,' Connie cried in response, the anguish in her voice was in complete contrast to the other two women.

Debra swung the gun towards Connie and the small woman gasped and subsided into silence. 'Kathy said to shut the fuck up.'

'This has to stop,' Willy bit out, turning towards his wife. 'Debs, we can't hide this any longer. *I* can't hide this any longer.' Debra shook her head, causing the gun to waver ominously.

'It's my brother,' John Dewer interrupted unexpectedly, nodding towards the shadowed corner where the remains still lay in their damp resting place.

'Your *brother*?' questioned the Admiral incredulously.

John shook his head. 'Like Connie said, there was an accident,' was all he offered in the end.

'So, naturally you cut him up and left him in a *cardboard box*...?'

'I said SHUT UP.' Debra shouted, waving the gun around wildly. Her anger was coloured with a tinge of madness and the Admiral realised she was on the verge of cracking. He stepped back as Pickles' growling got louder.

'For fuck's sake Debra, please. The guilt is crippling me. I don't know why you decided to come back, but you can't just turn up and think things can go back to the way they were.' Willy's voice was equally tormented and unexpectedly, her husband's desperation seemed to bring back Debra's control.

'It wasn't crippling you when you were raking the bloody money in though was it?' she said, her voice dripping with contempt. 'None of you felt any guilt then, did you?'

'That was different. Nobody had died then.'

'You think?' responded Debra with a humourless laugh. 'You're pathetic Will. You didn't even think about how many people might have died from the bloody drugs did you?'

The Admiral frowned, understanding suddenly dawning.

'You were peddling drugs.' he stated throwing all caution to the winds. He took a deep breath before continuing recklessly, 'You might as well tell me the rest of the sorry tale before you get rid of me. And while you're at it, what the bloody hell has Iris Denmead got to do with the whole cake and arse party. Was she in on it too?'

This time Kathy was the one who inhaled sharply.

'Stop talking Mr Shackleford,' she barked before turning back to Willy. 'It's no good losing your nerve Will. It's far too late for that. If the whole story goes public now, we'll all be spending the rest of our lives in jail. What happened *will* remain between these four walls.' Her last sentence was said in a voice devoid of any emotion. They were the most chilling words the Admiral had heard up to now. He realised that Debra and Kathy at least had no intention of letting him leave here alive.

'Come on Jimmy,' he muttered under his breath. It was one thing trying to goad the culprits into a bloody confession, but he might have dropped a bit of a bollock given that at least two of them were almost certainly a sandwich short of a picnic.

The Admiral was now struggling to hold Pickles back. Hastily he turned his attention back to John, the only one left with any seeming control, and tried a different tack., 'How did Jenny die John?' he asked softly, remembering the man's sadness when he'd spoken about Jenny Welbeck's death.

There was a sudden silence in the barn as though time had stopped. When John finally spoke, nobody tried to stop him.

'Jenny found out that her stepfather hadn't actually buried her mother under the patio or anywhere else.' He glanced over at

Debra who hadn't moved a muscle. 'She was devastated. Willy had told her over and over again that her mother left of her own accord. I think at the end of the day, she just couldn't handle the truth. I tried to stop her, but I was too late.' The Admiral could see actual tears sliding down the man's cheeks in the torchlight. 'My coat got caught in the bloody door,' he finished brokenly. 'I couldn't reach her in time. I just stood and watched her go over the edge.'

'So how come Iris and Jim Denmead found her?' asked the Admiral, almost convinced of the man's sincerity. John shook his head. 'A couple of days earlier I'd called Iris to tell her I was worried about Jenny's mental state and what she might do. Iris decided to book into the lighthouse for a few days in the hope she'd be able to meet up with Jenny and talk some sense into her. She never had the chance. Instead, I left her and Jim to find Jenny's broken body.'

'But I came back for her,' Debra wailed seeming to come out of her trance. 'I couldn't tell her why I'd left.'

'Because the truth is you got too damn greedy,' spat Connie venomously. 'With Ian dead, you knew the supply would dry up, so you took the stash and fucked off.'

Debra turned to the small woman, her voice back to calm. 'But I came back,' she repeated before lifting the shotgun and shooting Connie from point blank range.

The noise was deafening as Connie's body flew backwards with the impact. For a few seconds, shock held everyone immobile, then Debra turned back to the Admiral and took aim again.

At the same moment, an apparition dressed all in black suddenly materialised out of the shadows, brandishing something. For a horrible second, the Admiral truly thought it was the grim reaper coming to claim him, but the spectre shot past and threw itself at Debra who screamed in pure fear and fell backwards, causing the shotgun to fire up into the rafters. The Admiral let go of Pickles' lead and the spaniel launched himself at Debra who was now lying curled up on the floor with her eyes tightly shut moaning, 'I can't see, I can't see.'

'What the bloody hell?' spluttered the Admiral as the apparition turned back towards him and pushed back its hood. 'Talk about making a bloody meal of it Charlie Shackleford,' Mabel commented crossly.

Chapter Eighteen

T he police arrived only a couple of minutes later followed by an almost frantic Jimmy.

Apparently, the first gunshot had sounded just as the men were climbing out of the patrol car. The two officers had immediately set off at a run, leaving the former Master at Arms to follow on behind.

They arrived at the barn entrance just in time to witness Mabel's impressive impersonation of Death and on hearing the second gunshot, had stormed the building.

Once they'd assessed the risk, the officers blocked the entrance to the barn preventing anyone from leaving and immediately called for back-up. As Mabel was heard to remark later to her friends at the Women's Institute, 'It was just like an episode of Crime Scene Investigation...'

By ten pm, it was all over bar the shouting. After giving initial statements, the remaining members of Morwelly's very own drug cartel were handcuffed and taken away. All except the body of Connie Baxter which was still awaiting the forensic team.

And of course, Ian Dewer, whose remains had been on the verge of disappearing forever...

∞ ∞ ∞

The police informed them the next day that Willy Welbeck had fallen over himself to tell them everything once he'd been taken to the interview room at Exeter. He gave the police full details of their drug operations and the events leading up to Ian Dewer's death. It seemed his guilt far outstripped any sense of loyalty to his fellow conspirators.

All seven of the cartel - Kathy Brummel, Willy and Debra Welbeck, John and Ian Dewer, Connie Baxter and Iris Denmead had grown up together in Morwelly. However, both Debra and Ian had moved away, only to return some years later. Debra with a small, clearly unwanted daughter in tow, and Ian with a shady past that was threatening to catch up with him.

In the beginning, Ian had been bringing the drugs in for someone higher up the food chain - mostly to keep them from doing him serious injury. But at Willy and Debra's wedding, everything changed.

It turned out that Debra Welbeck had a head for business and few moral scruples. Once she found out about Ian's illegal drug dealings, not only did she want in, she also developed ideas to increase the amount they handled. Within two years, the amount of cocaine coming into north Devon had increased tenfold, much to the concern of the authorities.

Ian Dewer had the contacts. He, together with his brother John, Willy, Debra, and Connie used the tourist industry to cover up their activities. *Morwelly Cruises* proved very popular and it was easy to bring the drugs in to the small harbour and move them up country using Iris Denmead's 'Real Devon Ice Cream Company'. Jim Denmead knew nothing about it. A naïve primary school teacher, as far as he was concerned, his wife's choc ices was as good as anything made in Cornwall!

The whole operation had proved to be very profitable. So much so, it had provided the money for Connie to buy her beautiful chocolate box guesthouse, Kathy, her delightful tearooms. John a large imposing gothic pile with a view to die for and Iris and Jim an impressive stone manor house deep in the wilds of Dartmoor. Willy and Debra continued to live in the old farmhouse Willy had inherited from his parents. Debra told her husband it was better they save up the money until they had enough to retire to somewhere warm and sunny.

On the day of Ian's death, all seven had apparently been holding an impromptu celebration party on his boat Aphrodite to celebrate their first ten million. An argument between Debra and Ian had ensued and somehow Ian had fallen overboard in between the quayside and the boat. He'd been pinned in between the fender and the edge of the concrete berth and by the time they managed to fish him out, he was dead.

And so was their lucrative drug operation.

For a while, not knowing what else to do, they left Ian's body underneath a bunk on board his boat. Aphrodite slowly went to seed, as did Ian Dewer's remains buried inside. Nobody missed him - a loner with an unsavoury past. John simply told anyone who asked that his brother had decided to go abroad.

It had been Kathy's idea to chop up the body and get rid of each bit slowly to avoid suspicion.

As for Debra, once she finally realised that no Ian meant no more drug money, Willy's less than devoted wife decided to do a runner. Unfortunately, she chose to take their ill-gotten gains with her rather than her daughter.

The police asked Willy why he thought she'd decided to come back. It was the only question to which he had no answer.

'Bloody hell, I won't be sorry to see the back of these bollocking stairs,' muttered the Admiral as he carted the last suitcase down to the car.

'I have to admit they're more suited to someone with a little more stamina,' agreed Mabel following on behind.

'Or thirty years younger,' added Emily tartly.

'You're only as young as the case you're solving,' offered Jimmy jovially, still cock a hoop that they'd all emerged from *Operation Lighthouse* in one piece.

The Admiral grunted. 'Never thought I'd say this Jimmy lad, but I'll be glad to throw my towel in for a few months after this one. A nastier bunch of murdering psychopaths I've never come across.'

'Why, how many murdering psychopaths have you come across up to now Charlie?' commented Mabel, climbing into the car.

The Admiral hmphed and turned to lock the door and post the keys through the letterbox as they'd been instructed.

'Well, with a bit of luck Sir, we won't come into contact with any more psychopaths - murdering or otherwise - any time soon. And, anyway, tomorrow's Christmas Eve. It's officially the season of good will. We've got more important things to think about.'

'Well *you* certainly have Charlie Shackleford,' Mabel said, putting her arm around Pickles in the back seat. As soon as the sales start we'll be shopping for diamonds. I think a Spring wedding might be rather special. What do you think Emily?'

The End

The Admiral, Mabel, Jimmy and Emily will return ...

If you haven't yet read Books One and Two of The Admiral Shackleford Mysteries, *A Murderous Valentine and A Murderous Marriage* are available from Amazon.

Of course, if you haven't yet got around to reading The Dartmouth Diaries series and would like to know just how the Admiral was instrumental in getting his daughter Victory hitched to the most famous actor in the world, not to mention all his other shenanigans, all five books in the series are available on Amazon.

Claiming Victory: Book One

Sweet Victory: Book Two

All For Victory: Book Three

Chasing Victory: Book Four

Lasting Victory: Book Five

Continue reading to the end for an exclusive sneak peek of Claiming Victory, Book One...

Keeping in Touch

Thank you so much for reading *A Murderous Season* I really hope you enjoyed it.

For any of you who'd like to connect, I'd really love to hear from you. Feel free to contact me via my facebook page at https://www.facebook.com/beverleywattsauthor or my website at http://www.beverleywatts.com

If you'd like me to let you know as soon as my next book is released, sign up to my newsletter and I'll keep you updated about that and all my latest releases. Copy and paste the following link to sign up.

https://motivated-teacher-3299.ck.page/143a008c18

And lastly, thanks a million for taking the time to read this story. If you've read all about the Admiral's shenanigans in the earlier two Admiral Shackleford Mysteries, you might be interested to learn how the Admiral was instrumental in marrying off his only daughter to the most famous actor on the planet. You can read all about it in Book One of *The Dartmouth Diaries*. *Claiming Victory* is a funny contemporary romantic comedy that will appeal to every woman who still believes fairy tales can come true...

You might also be interested to learn that the Admiral's Great, Great, Great, Great, Great Grandfather appears in my latest series of lighthearted Regency Romances entitled The Shackleford Sisters.

Book One: *Grace*, Book Two: *Temperance*, Book Three: *Faith*, Book Four: *Hope*, Book Five: *Patience* and Book Six: *Charity* are currently available on Amazon with Book Seven: *Chastity* to be released on 25th May 2023.

Turn the page for a sneak peek of Claiming Victory - Book One of the Dartmouth Diaries...

Claiming Victory

'Victory Shackleford is a spinster, or at least well on the way to becoming one. She is thirty two years old, still lives with her father - an eccentric retired Admiral, and the love of her life is a dog.

She thinks her father is reckless, irresponsible, and totally incapable of looking after himself. He thinks his daughter is a boring nagging harpy with no imagination or sense of adventure and what's more, he's determined to get her married off.

Unfortunately there's no one in the picturesque yachting town of Dartmouth that Tory is remotely interested in, despite her father's best efforts.

But all that is about to change when she discovers that her madcap father has rented out their house as a location shoot for the biggest blockbuster of the year. As cast and crew descend, Tory's humdrum orderly existence is turned completely upside down, especially as the lead actor has just been voted the sexiest man on the planet...'

Chapter One

Retired Admiral, Charles Shackleford, entered the dimly lit interior of his favourite watering hole. Once inside, he waited a second for his eyes to adjust, and glanced around to check that his ageing Springer spaniel was already seated beside his stool at the bar. Pickles had disappeared into the undergrowth half a mile back, as they walked along the wooded trail high above the picturesque River Dart. The scent of some poor unfortunate rabbit had caught his still youthful nose. The Admiral was not unduly worried; this was a regular occurrence, and Pickles knew his way to the Ship Inn better than his master.

Satisfied that all was as it should be for a Friday lunchtime, Admiral Shackleford waved to the other regulars, and made his way to his customary seat at the bar where his long standing, and long suffering friend, Jimmy Noon, was already halfway down his first pint.

'You're a bit late today Sir,' observed Jimmy, after saluting his former commanding officer smartly.

Charles Shackleford grunted as he heaved his ample bottom onto the bar stool. 'Got bloody waylaid by that bossy daughter of mine.' He sighed dramatically before taking a long draft of his pint of real ale, which was ready and waiting for him. 'Damn bee in her bonnet since she found out about my relationship with Mabel Pomfrey. Of course, I told her to mind her own bloody business, but it has to be said that the cat's out of the bag, and no mistake.'

He stared gloomily down into his pint. 'She said it cast aspersions on her poor mother's memory. But what she doesn't understand Jimmy, is that I'm still a man in my prime. I've got needs. I mean look at me – why can't she see that I'm still a fine figure of a man, and any woman would be more than happy to shack up with me.'

Abruptly, the Admiral turned towards his friend so the light shone directly onto his face and leaned forward. 'Come on then man, tell me you agree.'

Jimmy took a deep breath as he dubiously regarded the watery eyes, thread veined cheeks, and larger than average nose no more than six inches in front of him

However, before he could come up with a suitably acceptable reply that wouldn't result in him standing to attention for the next four hours in front of the Admiral's dishwasher, the Admiral turned away, either indicating it was purely a rhetorical question, or he genuinely couldn't comprehend that anyone could possibly regard him as less than a prime catch.

Jimmy sighed with relief. He really hadn't got time this afternoon to do dishwasher duty as he'd agreed to take his wife shopping.

Although to be fair, a four hour stint in front of an electrical appliance at the Admiral's house, with Tory sneaking him tea and biscuits, was actually preferable to four hours trailing after his wife in Marks and Spencer's. He didn't think his wife would see it that way though. Emily Noon had enough trouble understanding her husband's tolerance towards 'that dinosaur's' eccentricities as it was.

Of course, Emily wasn't aware that only the quick thinking of the dinosaur in question had, early on in their naval career, saved her husband from a potentially horrible fate involving a Thai prostitute who'd actually turned out to be a man...

As far as Jimmy was concerned, Admiral Shackleford was his Commanding Officer, and always would be, and if that involved such idiosyncrasies as presenting himself in front of a dishwasher with headphones on, saluting and saying, 'Dishwasher manned and ready sir.' Then four hours later, saluting again while saying, 'Dishwasher secured,' so be it.

It was a small price to pay...

He leaned towards his morose friend and patted him on the back, showing a little manly support (acceptable, even from subordinates), while murmuring, 'Don't worry about it too much Sir. Tory's a sensible girl. She'll come round eventually – you know she wants you to be happy.' The Admiral's only response was an inelegant snort, so Jimmy ceased his patting, and went back to his pint.

Both men gazed into their drinks for a few minutes, as if all the answers would be found in the amber depths.

'What she needs is a man.' Jimmy's abrupt observation drew another rude snort, this one even louder.

'Who do you suggest? She's not interested in anyone. Says there's no one in Dartmouth she'd give house room to, and believe me I've tried. When she's not giving me grief, she spends all her time in that bloody gallery with all those airy fairy types. Can't imagine any one of them climbing her rigging. Not one set of balls between 'em.' Jimmy chuckled at the Admiral's description of Tory's testosterone challenged male friends.

'She's not ugly though,' Charles Shackleford mused, still staring into his drink. 'She might have an arse the size of an aircraft carrier, but she's got her mother's top half which balances it out nicely.'

'Aye, she's built a bit broad across the beam,' Jimmy agreed nodding his head.

'And then there's this bloody film crew. I haven't told her yet.' Jimmy frowned at the abrupt change of subject and shot a puzzled glance over to the Admiral.

'Film crew? What film crew?'

Charles Shackleford looked back irritably. 'Come on Jimmy, get a grip. I'm talking about that group of nancies coming to film at the house next month. I must have mentioned it.'

Jimmy simply shook his head in bewilderment.

Frowning at his friend's obtuseness, the Admiral went on, 'You know, what's that bloody film they're making at the moment – big blockbuster everyone's talking about?'

'What, you mean The Bridegroom?'

'That's the one. Seems like they were looking for a large house overlooking the River Dart. Think they were hoping for Greenway, you know, Agatha Christie's place, but then they spied "the Admiralty" and said it was spot on. Paying me a packet they are. Coming next week.'

Jimmy stared at his former commanding officer with something approaching pity. 'And you've arranged all this without telling Tory?'

'None of her bloody business,' the Admiral blustered, banging his now empty pint glass on the bar, and waving at the barmaid for a refill. 'She's out most of the time anyway.'

Jimmy shook his head in disbelief. 'When are you going to tell her?'

'Was going to do it this morning, but then this business with Mabel came up so I scarpered. Last I saw she was taking that bloody little mongrel of hers out for a walk. Hoping she'll walk off her temper.' His tone indicated he considered there was more likelihood of hell freezing over.

'Is Noah Westbrook coming?' said Jimmy, suddenly sensing a bit of gossip he could pass on to Emily.

'Noah who?' was the Admiral's bewildered response.

'Noah Westbrook. Come on Sir, you must know him. He's the most famous actor in the world. Women go completely gaga over him. If nothing else, that should make Tory happy.'

The Admiral stared at him thoughtfully. 'What's he look like, this Noah West... chappy?'

The barmaid, who had been unashamedly listening to the whole conversation, couldn't contain herself any longer and, thrusting a glossy magazine under the Admiral's nose, said breathlessly, 'Like this. He looks like this.'

The full colour photograph was that of a naked man lounging on a sofa, with only a towel protecting his modesty, together with the caption "Noah Westbrook, officially voted the sexiest man on the planet."

Admiral Charles Shackleford stared pensively down at the picture in front of him. 'So this Noah chap – he's in this film is he?'

'He's got the lead role.' The bar maid actually twittered causing the Admiral to look up in irritation – bloody woman must be fifty if she's a day. Shooting her a withering look, he went back to the magazine, and read the beginning of the article inside.

"Noah Westbrook is to be filming in the South West of England over the next month, causing a sudden flurry of bookings to hotels and guest houses in the South Devon area."

The Admiral continued to stare at the photo, the germination of an idea tiptoeing around the edges of his brain. Glancing up, he discovered he was the subject of scrutiny from not just the barmaid, but now the whole pub was waiting with bated breath to hear what he was going to say next.

The Admiral's eyes narrowed as the beginnings of a plan slowly began taking shape, but he needed to keep it under wraps. Looking around at his rapt audience, he feigned nonchalance. 'Don't think Noah Westbrook was mentioned at all in the correspondence. Think he must be filming somewhere else.'

Then, without saying anything further, he downed the rest of his drink, and climbed laboriously off his stool.

'Coming Jimmy, Pickles?' His tone was deceptively casual which fooled Jimmy not at all, and, sensing something momentous afoot, the smaller man swiftly finished his pint. In his haste to follow the Admiral out of the door, he only narrowly avoided falling over Pickles who, completely unappreciative of the need for urgency, was sitting in the middle of the floor, scratching unconcernedly behind his ear.

Once outside, the Admiral didn't bother waiting for his dog, secure in the knowledge that someone would let the elderly spaniel out before he got too far down the road. Instead, he took hold of Jimmy's arm, and dragged him out of earshot – just in case anyone was listening.

In complete contrast to his mood on arrival, Charles Shackleford was now grinning from ear to ear. 'That's it. I've finally got a plan,' he hissed to his bewildered friend. 'I'm going to get her married off.'

'Who to?' asked Jimmy confused.

'Don't be so bloody slow Jimmy. To him of course. The actor chappy, Noah Westbrook. According to that magazine, women everywhere fall over themselves for him. Even Victory won't be able to resist him.'

Jimmy opened his mouth but nothing came out. He stared in complete disbelief as the Admiral went on. 'Then she'll move out, and Mabel can move in. Simple.'

Pickles came ambling up as Jimmy finally found his voice. 'So, let me get this straight Sir. Your plan is to somehow get Noah Westbrook, the most famous actor on the entire planet to fall in love with your daughter Victory, who we both love dearly, but - and please don't take offence Sir - who you yourself admit is built generously across the aft, and whose face is unlikely to launch the Dartmouth ferry, let alone a thousand ships.'

The Admiral frowned. 'Well admittedly, I've not worked out the finer details, but that's about the sum of it. What do you think...?'

Claiming Victory is available on Amazon.

Books available on Amazon

The Dartmouth Diaries:

Book 1 - Claiming Victory
Book 2 - Sweet Victory
Book 3 - All for Victory
Book 4 - Chasing Victory
Book 5 - Lasting Victory

The Admiral Shackleford Mysteries

Book 1 - A Murderous Valentine
Book 2 - A Murderous Marriage
Book 3 - A Murderous Season

The Shackleford Sisters

Book 1 - Grace
Book 2 - Temperance
Book 3 - Faith
Book 4 - Hope
Book 5 - Patience
Book 6 - Charity
Book 7 - Chastity
Book 8 - Prudence to be released on 31st August 2023

Standalone Titles

An Officer and a Gentleman Wanted

About The Author

Beverley Watts

Beverley spent 8 years teaching English as a Foreign Language to International Military Students in Britannia Royal Naval College, the Royal Navy's premier officer training establishment in the UK. She says that in the whole 8 years there was never a dull moment and many of her wonderful experiences at the College were not only memorable but were most definitely 'the stuff of fiction.' Her debut novel An Officer

And A Gentleman Wanted is very loosely based on her adventures at the College.

Beverley particularly enjoys writing books that make people laugh and currently she has two series of Romantic Comedies, both contemporary and historical, as well as a humorous cosy mystery series under her belt.

She lives with her husband in an apartment overlooking the sea on the beautiful English Riviera. Between them they have 3 adult children and two gorgeous grandchildren plus a menagerie of animals including 5 dogs - 3 Romanian rescues of indeterminate breed called Florence, Trixie, and Lizzie, a neurotic 'Chorkie' named Pepé and a 'Chichon" named Dotty who was the inspiration for Dotty in The Dartmouth Diaries.

You can find out more about Beverley's books at www.beverleywatts.com

Printed in Great Britain
by Amazon

32394634R00066